For Letter or Worse

Margaret Welch

AnniesFiction.com

Books in the Secrets of the Castleton Manor Library series

A Novel Murder
Bitter Words
The Grim Reader
A Deadly Chapter
An Autographed Mystery
Second Edition Death
A Crime Well Versed
A Murder Unscripted
Pride and Publishing
A Literary Offense
Up to Noir Good
For Letter or Worse
On Pens and Needles
Ink or Swim
Tell No Tales
Page Fright
A Fatal Yarn
Read Between the Crimes
From Fable to Grave
A Fateful Sentence
Cloak and Grammar
A Lost Clause
A Thorny Plot
A Scary Tale Wedding

For Letter or Worse
Copyright © 2018, 2022 Annie's.

All rights reserved. No part of this publication may be reproduced, stored in a retrieval system, or transmitted in any form or by any means—electronic, mechanical, photocopying, recording or otherwise—without the prior written permission of the publisher. The only exception is brief quotations in printed reviews. For information address Annie's, 306 East Parr Road, Berne, Indiana 46711-1138.

The characters and events in this book are fictional, and any resemblance to actual persons or events is coincidental.

Library of Congress-in-Publication Data
For Letter or Worse/ by Margaret Welch
p. cm.
I. Title
                    2018932477

AnniesFiction.com
(800) 282-6643
Secrets of the Castleton Manor Library™
Series Creator: Shari Lohner
Series Editor: Lorie Jones
Cover Illustrator: Jesse Reisch

10 11 12 13 14 | Printed in South Korea | 9 8 7 6 5

Faith Newberry joined her black-and-white tuxedo cat at one of the windows in the Castleton Manor library.

From a pool of sunshine, Watson blinked up at her.

She leaned down and rubbed the purr spot between his ears. "There goes a blue Mustang convertible. It's sleek and sporty—just like you."

The Mustang wasn't nearly as old as some of the cars she'd seen that afternoon, but she guessed it was an early model from the sixties. Along with other vintage cars, it rolled up to Castleton Manor, bringing guests to the Nancy Drew Clue Colloquium, a gathering of scholars and fans of the girl detective.

Serious fans, Faith realized, if they sought out, bought, and drove the cars a character had owned throughout her decades-long fictional career.

As Faith rubbed the cat between his ears again, she smiled at the thought of him behind the wheel of the Mustang, whiskers swept back, cruising down the highway. "Well, maybe I should drive, Watson, but you can have dibs on riding shotgun."

The library was the perfect vantage point for catching glimpses of people arriving at the château-style mansion in Lighthouse Bay, Massachusetts.

That Faith's cherished cat was welcome at the pet-friendly manor was one of the perks of her job. The job itself—librarian and archivist—was a dream come true. Every day she felt grateful for the chance she'd had to leave a more stressful position as an academic librarian in Boston and move to the seaside town on Cape Cod.

The late-September sun glinted off the shiny, deep maroon of another antique car on its way to the manor. Nancy Drew had driven a maroon roadster in a couple of the early books. One of them even had a rumble seat.

Faith glanced at Watson. In addition to other unusual traits her rescue cat had, he liked riding in cars. She'd always wanted to ride in a rumble seat. Maybe he'd like that too.

"Oh! Do you see that next car, Watson? That has to be a roadster. A blue roadster, exactly like the one Nancy had in *The Secret of the Old Clock*. Forget rumble seats and Mustangs. Your elegant fur tuxedo was made for riding in that machine. If we had that car, you and I would tool around the back roads solving mysteries left and right. Wouldn't that be the life?"

She felt a little silly gushing over the car to her cat. Of course she talked to him. What pet owner didn't talk to her pet? But Faith could always tell when the end of a quiet weekend approached, because she caught herself having longer conversations with Watson. Not that he seemed to mind. And not that he joined the conversations. Although there were times when he looked as though he might be thinking about what she'd said.

Watson was looking at her now, his head tipped slightly as though contemplating something—more likely his supper than blue roadsters.

"It isn't suppertime yet," Faith reminded him.

Watson yawned, stretched, and walked to the library's French doors.

"On the other hand, another dose of fresh air is a wonderful idea."

They'd started the afternoon with a bit of a ramble in the woods and then dropped by the library so Faith could find a book to identify a bird she hadn't recognized. She'd ended up getting lost in John James Audubon's essays, and Watson had taken up car watching.

Now, before following him out the door to the tiled terrace, Faith slipped into the tweed blazer she'd draped over the back of a chair. The sun was bright, but autumn had arrived the week before and there was a salt-tinged chill in the air.

Watson stopped and sniffed the cool air, then trotted down the terrace stairs, heading toward the Victorian garden.

There were several themed gardens on the manor's spacious grounds, and the Victorian garden, with its winding pathways and stone benches, was one of Faith's favorites. It was a pleasant place to sit and read, or in Watson's case, take a snooze in the sun.

At his age, Watson deserved all the sun-soaked naps he wanted. He seemed to agree, although he was still plenty spry and graceful despite having lost most of his tail in an accident when he was a kitten. He had the uncanny ability to appear in places, including rooms in the manor, seemingly out of thin air. Faith had learned that cat-proof wasn't the same as Watson-proof.

A nap might be on the cat's agenda now instead of a walk. Faith saw his bobbed-tail hind end disappear down one of the fieldstone paths. Then she turned as she heard the crunch of tires on gravel.

Another vintage car was arriving. It was green and black with a hardtop, running boards, and spoked wheels.

The driver, catching sight of her, waved and tooted the horn. It wasn't an *ooga* horn, but it definitely had the sound of a bygone era.

Faith waved back and then considered her options. On one hand, she wasn't expected to be working in the library today, and no one needed her assistance in welcoming the guests, checking them into their suites, and signing them in at the colloquium's registration tables.

On the other hand, as the librarian she could spend as much time in the manor as she wanted. She loved books and everything about them. She particularly loved mysteries. And as a child she'd read every Nancy Drew book she could get her hands on. She would see the guests all week and could certainly wait until tomorrow, but . . .

She glanced down at herself. Her corduroy trousers, cable-knit sweater, and tweed jacket weren't part of her everyday professional attire, but she thought they were presentable enough.

And she was itching to see if the drivers of those 1930s cars had dressed the part.

"Don't pinch me," a woman said to her companion as they stared up at the ceiling in Castleton Manor's magnificent two-story main lobby. "I've gone back in time, and I want to stay."

Faith smiled at the women. She knew that awed feeling well. The marble, gold leaf, exotic wood inlays, and crystal—from the gleaming floors, to the sweeping stairways, to the immense chandeliers, and on up to the ceiling—were enough to dazzle anyone.

Every time Faith stepped through the doors, she could imagine she'd been swept back to the turn of the last century. The mansion built by the wealthy shipowner Angus Jaxon could easily have been turned into a museum of Gilded Age history.

This afternoon the lobby echoed with the excitement of guests greeting each other like long-lost friends.

Or in keeping with the Nancy Drew spirit, maybe they think of themselves as long-lost chums, Faith thought.

She overheard one guest ask another in hushed tones if she'd seen her room yet and heard another ask her companion if she'd spotted Wolfe Jaxon. Faith knew they'd get their chance to catch sight of Castleton Manor's co-owner when he returned from a business trip to Chicago the next day.

A woman who appeared to be about forty stopped in front of Faith. "I don't think we've met. I'm Paloma Martin." She put her hand out.

Faith smiled and shook the woman's hand. "Faith Newberry. Welcome to Castleton Manor."

"You work here?" Paloma asked, giving her the once-over.

Faith realized her corduroy trousers and jacket might not measure up after all. "My day off," she said by way of explanation.

"Oh, I didn't mean to suggest what you're wearing—"

Faith laughed. "Don't worry. Actually, I just stopped by to see what all of *you* are wearing. I was kind of hoping to spot at least one or two Nancy Drews. But so far everyone looks—"

"Ordinary?" Paloma finished for her. "Now it's my turn to say don't worry. Most of us are still in traveling clothes. The colloquium doesn't officially start until predinner cocktails at six, but from that point on, we're encouraging everyone to get their Nancy Drew on. You'll see Nancies from the thirties, the forties, and on up through her modern incarnations. Some of our regulars go all out."

Faith laughed. "I can't wait to see."

"Many attendees were especially excited about your liberal pet policy," Paloma remarked. "I know of at least three people bringing their dogs—all named Togo after Nancy's dog, of course—and Bea Stapleton brought her cat, Snowball."

"I'm looking forward to meeting the rest of the guests and their pets," Faith said.

Paloma smiled as she caught sight of someone behind Faith. She raised her arm and waved, but all of a sudden, her hand dropped and her smile vanished. "You've got to be kidding me."

"Is something wrong?" Faith asked.

Her words were drowned out by twin shrieks coming from opposite ends of the lobby.

Faith whipped around to see two women running toward each other, their arms wide, and still shrieking what now sounded like "Nancy! Nancy!"

One of the women had a fox terrier that yipped and ran too until they all met in the middle. Then the women threw their arms around each other, and the dog ran in circles around both of them until he'd run out of leash and the women were bound together.

Two other dogs in the lobby joined in the happy barking.

"Togo, sit," the woman in the middle who was holding the leash commanded. "Sit."

The other two dogs sat. The dog in the middle stood on his hind legs. Laughing, the women disentangled themselves.

Faith had been prepared to offer assistance, but seeing that they were all right, she turned to Paloma, only to find Paloma gone and a man standing there in her place.

The man looked as amused by the situation as the women did. "Nancy said they cause a stir wherever they go," he said, motioning to the two women. "She was right again."

"Again?" Faith asked.

"Again and always. That's what she tells me, anyway, and she had your friend pegged. Did you see her face when they squealed? The only word for it is *prune*." The man held up his hands. "Don't get me wrong. I don't mean to offend. I have nothing against your friend. I don't even know her. But Nancy told me about her. They've got this rivalry thing going. It's all in good fun, but she told me to watch Ms. Prune's face when they did their gag. Ha! It was great."

Faith was rarely at a loss for polite words, but she struggled after this man's comments. And had those two women—who looked to be in their forties—really orchestrated the running and shrieking just to get at Paloma? "Is her name really Nancy?" she finally asked. It was the best she could come up with.

"They're both Nancy. Isn't that a crazy coincidence? The Nancy with the terrier is my fiancée. And I'm Vic Flynn, by the way." He suddenly shifted his gaze from the two Nancies to Faith. "So, are you here for this shindig?"

"No, I—"

"Just gawking? I hear you." His gaze shifted again, taking in the opulent lobby. "There's plenty to gawk at. Have you seen the dining room? They didn't do anything halfway when they built this place, that's for sure. Did you notice the antique cars and my sweet blue roadster?"

Faith opened her mouth but closed it again because Vic hadn't paused and possibly hadn't taken a breath.

"Each car gets its own garage here. Well, practically its own. They're all connected, like a Philadelphia row house, if you know what I mean, but classier than that. Of course, we're paying plenty for all that class. So, on the open market, how much do you think a place like this goes—" He stopped abruptly when the Nancy holding the dog's leash waved to get his attention.

"Vic, come on over here," she called. "Come say hi to Nancy. Then you can help with the bags and take Togo for a walk."

Without another word or glance in Faith's direction, Vic rushed to do his Nancy's bidding.

An elderly woman who'd been standing behind Vic offered a quiet chuckle. "He's better trained than that rascal of a dog," she said. "And if the rest of our week turns out to be as entertaining as that entrance, we're in for a grand time, don't you think?"

"I certainly hope so," Faith said.

"I, for one, am counting on it." The woman had a cane with her. She planted it firmly on the floor and rested her hands on the crook with a sigh. "There's only one problem so far."

"How can I help?" Faith asked.

"I've gotten myself turned around. I started off well enough by finding the library. That was my first goal, but then it teased me by being closed."

"I'm so sorry," Faith said. "I'll have it open tomorrow morning."

"Ah. Are you, by chance, the librarian?"

"Yes, I'm Faith Newberry."

"Very nice to meet you. I'm Lois who sometimes gets lost. I'll find my way back to see you in the library tomorrow, but in the meantime, can you tell me how to find the salon? That's where we register and pick up our programs and name badges and, most exciting, our swag bags."

"Of course," Faith said.

"You can just point me in the right direction." Lois frowned. "Although I have to admit, that's what I said to the last person who tried to get me there."

"Why don't I walk with you?" Faith suggested.

"Thank you. That will be lovely. We'll find it together." Lois took Faith by the arm. "I've already been to several places I didn't mean to go."

The cat, roused from his dreams, cast a disparaging look at the squirrel responsible for his shortened nap. In his estimation, squirrels should be chased and not heard chattering incessantly about the acorns they buried and lost track of.

He sniffed the air and glanced toward the snug cottage that he and his human shared. He could tell she hadn't returned yet. He left the garden and crossed the lawn to the manor, allowing a human who smelled of sand and sea wrack to open the door for him.

Upon entering the manor, the cat became aware of a situation that required his immediate attention—an invasion of dogs.

After making a quick and slinking reconnaissance circuit of the lobby and adjacent rooms, he concluded that there were now three fox terriers in residence, two bull terriers, and one Skye terrier—and they were all answering (or not, as the case so often was with dogs) to the same name. How singular! Dogs often came to stay at Castleton but usually in a wider variety of breeds and showing more creativity in their given names.

But while investigating the depth and breadth of the invasion of identically named dogs, the cat made a discovery far more interesting than any yip or woof could suggest. He encountered a delectable scent and a few long, white tail hairs.

These clues hinted at the presence of a newly arrived cat, most likely an enchanting creature more sophisticated than any of the dogs.

She was no doubt taking a nap somewhere stylish—a more appropriate activity than leaping, prancing, or sitting vapidly with her tongue hanging out—for she was certainly nowhere to be seen.

Faith could have pointed Lois toward the salon. It was only a short walk away. But she knew how easy it was for guests to get turned around during the first few days of a visit, and saving steps and more frustration for Lois would be a kindness. She was also interested in seeing how registration for the colloquium was going.

As she and Lois made their way there, they saw Brooke Milner, Faith's friend and sous-chef at the manor. She stood at the foot of the majestic staircase holding a baking tray.

"Stop right there, will you?" Brooke called from ten or fifteen feet away. "Now you two tell me if this is working." She walked forward, waving a cloth over the tray and wafting the air toward them. "What do you smell?"

"Crab cakes," Faith blurted out.

Brooke squawked.

"Do you?" Lois looked concerned. "I smell cookies."

Brooke removed the cloth with a flourish, revealing what was on the plate.

"They are cookies," Lois announced.

"And they smell delicious," Faith said. "I'm sorry about the crab cake remark. I was channeling my inner Watson, and you know how he loves your crab cakes." She introduced Brooke to her companion. "So what's the experiment? What are you up to?"

"I'm laying down a scent trail so the guests can follow their noses to Nancy Drew central." Brooke pointed toward the salon. "And so they find the refreshments. This is just a decoy tray, though. I'll take them back to the kitchen and frost them when they're cool enough."

"You mean we don't get to have one?" Lois asked.

"Wait until you see—and taste—the finished product," Brooke said, kissing her fingertips. "There are plenty, along with tea and coffee in the salon."

Faith suddenly heard a noise that sounded like a low moan. She moved around the side of the stairway.

"What are you doing?" Brooke called.

"I heard something."

Brooke and Lois followed.

When Faith heard the noise again, she pointed at the wainscoting. "There. Did you hear that?"

"No," Brooke said.

Faith felt something brush her ankle. "Hello, Watson. Did you hear something?"

Watson looked up at her and blinked.

"I heard it," Lois said. "And *that* was not mentioned in the brochure."

"What wasn't mentioned?" Brooke asked.

Lois clapped. "A haunted staircase!"

"Haunted?" Brooke raised her eyebrows and stared at Faith.

"Absolutely," Lois said. "I distinctly heard a moan. It was low and unearthly."

"Where's the ghost?" someone asked.

Faith turned to the newcomer and recognized her as one of the women named Nancy. "I'm sure there's another explanation—"

"It's in the staircase," Lois cut in. "Oh, this is so extraordinarily Drewian."

"And completely excellent," Nancy said. She ran up four or five steps of the grand staircase and produced a loud and startling whistle with two fingers in her mouth. "Your attention, please!"

The few guests still in the lobby turned to her.

Nancy beamed. "I am thrilled to announce that Castleton Manor, perfect in every way, is now even more perfect and truly Drew, because we have a haunted staircase!"

"Oh no," Brooke muttered under her breath. "Marlene is not going to be happy about this."

"Is she here today?" Faith asked.

"Yes, and I'm skedaddling back to the kitchen before she shows up, as you and I both know she surely will."

Faith regretted her prickly relationship with Marlene Russell, the manor's assistant manager, and she did her best to smooth over rough patches when they occurred. She tried not to sigh now, but she suspected that guests announcing the discovery of a haunted staircase, no matter how Drewian that might sound, could very easily turn into one of those rough patches.

Nancy and three other guests now stood with their ears to the wall, listening intently. Lois joined them.

One of the guests knocked on the wall. "I heard something answer. Did anyone else hear it?"

The others shook their heads.

"We might have scared it," Nancy said with a wink at Faith. "But it wouldn't be much of a ghost if it answered on demand. Come on. Let's leave the poor moaning thing in peace."

Faith wondered about that wink, but she was glad when the other women laughed over their so-called ghostly experience and followed Nancy away.

Lois stayed behind with Faith. "I started a bit of a to-do, didn't I?" She patted Faith's arm. "I'm sure you're used to dealing with all kinds of things, though."

"Oh yes. All kinds," Faith assured her.

Marlene marched over to them. "What on earth is going on?"

Watson was the first to greet Marlene, sauntering over and twining around the ankles of her black trousers.

Even though Castleton's guests were encouraged to bring their companions with them for an indulgent stay, Marlene had a low tolerance for animals. But she'd grudgingly come to accept Watson—just barely.

"You have an admirer," Lois said.

"How does he do that?" Marlene asked. "When I wear light-colored pants, he seems to only shed his white fur on them. When I wear black, he only leaves the black. It's uncanny, and frankly, I wouldn't put up with his behavior otherwise." She turned to Faith. "Call him away now and explain this nonsense I heard about a haunted staircase. We don't need our guests believing wild stories like that."

"It might not be a ghost, but it isn't nonsense," Lois said. "I heard it myself." She wiggled her fingers at Watson. "Come on over here, Mr. Handsome. We'll leave these two clever ladies to sort it out."

The elderly human with the kind look in her eye attempted to attract the cat's attention by wiggling her fingers and making nonsensical cooing noises.

The cat would have considered showing his own kindness by letting her know that her wool skirt smelled disturbingly of mothballs. But she was obviously a poor creature with limited language abilities and only a slim chance of understanding his communications.

Encountering such people no longer surprised him, but it remained a source of disappointment to him. But that disappointment wasn't as profound as when his own human didn't offer him more than a pawful of crunchy tunaroons for a snack.

Deciding it was better not to engage and far more interesting to investigate the ghost in the staircase, he ignored the elderly human and went to examine the wainscoting. The essence of mothballs trailed after him, making him sneeze. Or perhaps it was the other scent lingering near the baseboard that tickled his nose. He sneezed again.

And heard an answering sound from the staircase.

"Why is your cat staring at the wall like that?" Marlene asked. "And why is he sneezing? Is he sick? Is he hurt?"

Faith knelt beside her pet. She didn't think Watson was sick, but she put the back of her hand to his nose.

Watson gave her a reassuring, slow cat blink. Then he meowed.

A soft sound came from behind the baseboard.

"Aha. Clever Watson. That's what I thought too." Faith turned to Marlene and Lois. "We don't have a ghost. We have a cat in the wainscoting. It must have gotten into one of the hidden passageways." She put her head near the baseboard and called, "Kitty?"

A muffled, moaning sort of mew came in reply.

Marlene brought out her key ring. "I'd like to know whose cat this is and exactly how it got there." She separated a skeleton key from the others on the ring and showed them a hidden door in the corner where the staircase met the wall.

"Poor baby," Lois said. "I hope it's close by."

"Watson's still here," Faith said, "so I expect the other cat is too."

Marlene fitted the key into a well-disguised keyhole. She tugged the door gently, and it swung open.

A cat with long white hair strolled out without fuss.

"It might not be a real ghost, but it's as white as one," Lois remarked.

Watson greeted the rescued cat with a friendly meow.

The cat sauntered right past him.

"She doesn't act like a ghost," Faith said. "She didn't say boo to Watson."

"How do you know it's a she?" Marlene asked as she closed the door and relocked it.

"I think this might be Bea Stapleton's cat, Snowball." Faith stooped and held her hand out to the cat. "How did you get shut in there, sweet girl? Why didn't you yowl or meow louder so someone could let you out sooner? We should find Bea and tell her—"

"Tell me what?"

Faith looked up and saw a tall silver-haired woman in her sixties with blue eyes. She recognized Bea Stapleton—the president of the Nancy Drew Clue Society—from photographs she'd seen.

The white cat saved Faith the trouble of answering Bea by mewing the news of her imprisonment pitifully.

Faith thought the cat might be exaggerating the situation, considering how calm, cool, and collected her behavior had been moments before, but she forgave the cat because she didn't know all the details.

As far as she knew, Bea didn't know *any* of the details, but that didn't stop her from scooping the cat into her arms as though rescuing her pet from molten lava and then erupting herself when Marlene started filling her in.

"First, I want to know how Snowball got out of my suite." Bea turned to a young man in his twenties who'd been hanging back.

"Drew, was she in the suite when you left?"

"Yes, she was asleep on the window seat," the young man said promptly.

"As I thought." Bea snapped back around to Marlene. "Second, I want to know how she ended up in your hidden passageway. Third would be to ask why she wasn't found sooner, but as we don't know how long she was gone, that part of the discussion will be tabled until we do."

"We will answer all your questions as best we can," Marlene said, "and you have my sincerest apology for this mishap. Please let us know if Snowball has been harmed in any way. We have a concierge veterinarian who can be here at a moment's notice. As for how long she was behind the staircase, I don't think—"

"Behind the staircase?" Bea held Snowball to her cheek and glanced toward the salon. "I think I see. I'm beginning to understand."

"Do you know what happened?" Faith asked.

"I have a very good idea, but unlike some, I won't stoop to spreading unfounded rumors," Bea said, then addressed the young man. "Please take Snowball back up to the suite. Keep an eye on her for a while, will you? See if she has any appetite." She handed the cat to him.

"Your grandson?" Marlene asked as he started up the staircase.

"My son." Bea sounded both frosty and defensive.

Marlene briefly looked mortified for her faux pas. She recovered soon enough, but Faith knew she hated offending or embarrassing guests, no matter how inadvertently.

Bea must have noticed Marlene's discomfort too because she said, "Forgive my bad temper. It has nothing to do with you and your perfectly understandable question." Her hand went to the silver locket at her throat. "Drew is my adopted son, and I am old enough to be his grandmother. Every day I thank God for bringing him into my life."

They watched Bea go, and then Faith said, "I wonder what she thinks happened."

"And if she intends to do anything about it," Lois added. "She seemed very fierce."

"Well, that's all I need to complicate this week," Marlene groused. "Mysteries and amateur sleuths. If you find out how that cat got into the passage, Faith, I want to know." She stalked off.

Watson followed Marlene.

"You behave yourself, Watson," Faith called after him.

Before he went around a corner after Marlene, it looked as though he winked at her.

It must have been a trick of the light. Faith gave herself a mental shake and turned back to Lois. "Are you ready to go register?"

"I should have saved you the trouble and gone with Bea." Lois took Faith's arm. "But so far we've been having excellent adventures, so I'm happy sticking with you. Plus, we might be lucky enough to find your friend's cookies."

The salon, though large and one of Faith's favorite rooms at the manor, wasn't as immense or posh as the library or the Great Hall Gallery. It provided a more intimate space for author interviews, cooking demonstrations, dance lessons, and occasional movies.

When Faith and Lois entered the salon, Bea and Paloma sat behind the registration table.

Two women stood on the other side of the table, each with a blue tote bag over her shoulder, and the two women named Nancy waited in line with the fox terrier.

With a shared conspiratorial look, Faith and Lois made a beeline for the refreshment table and helped themselves. Brooke's cookies were cut in the shape of the classic Nancy Drew silhouette and iced in blue.

"Perfection," Lois said after taking a bite of one.

Faith agreed.

"You purposely changed the date!" the Nancy with the dog shouted. The dog yipped as if in agreement.

When her fellow Nancy put a hand on her shoulder, Faith assumed it was to calm her.

But then the second Nancy lashed out as well. "You absolutely did it on purpose. Hasn't this colloquium always met in October to celebrate Edward Stratemeyer's birthday? Hasn't it?"

"It has," Bea said.

"That's funny because this seems to be September," the second Nancy sneered. "You thought changing the date would keep us away."

Before Bea could respond, the first Nancy chimed in, "Don't bother to deny it. The River Heights Roundtable has a legitimate bone to pick with you, and we're the two who intend to do the picking."

Lois looked startled and put a hand on Faith's arm.

Faith gave her what she hoped was a reassuring smile. She thought about calling Marlene, but instead she picked up the tray of cookies and headed for the table and the squabbling women. Defusing the situation with refreshments and humor might do the trick.

With feigned breeziness, Faith pushed between the two Nancies and spoke to the fox terrier first. "Hello, sweetie. What a good dog. Let me guess. Your name is Togo, right?"

The dog wagged his tail.

She smiled at the four women. "Hello, I'm Faith Newberry, the librarian here at Castleton. Has anyone offered these adorable cookies to you?"

Bea declined, but Paloma and both Nancies accepted the cookies.

The Nancy with the dog winked at Faith.

Faith did a double take and wondered if it was a trick of the light or if it was another gag like Vic had talked about.

"Nancy Allerton, otherwise known as Nancy A." She held her hand out to Faith as she glanced at her dog. "Shake."

Her dog lifted his paw.

Faith shook Nancy's hand, then stooped to shake the paw, being careful to keep the tray of cookies at a safe distance from the dog.

"And I'm Nancy Ziegler. Nancy Z. to my besties," the other Nancy said with a smirk at the women behind the registration table. "Nancy and I didn't actually meet out there in the lobby." She glanced at her hand, wiped it quickly on Nancy A.'s sleeve, and held it out.

Faith shook it.

Both Nancies hooted with laughter.

"We're the founding and possibly the only members of the River Heights Roundtable. Experts on Nancy D."—Nancy Z. pointed at Nancy A., then herself—"from A to Z."

"Despite the subterfuge that almost kept us from attending," Nancy A. said, peering over the top of her red glasses and giving Bea and Paloma a sour look, "we plan to have a fantastic, fabulous, gargantuan time while we're here."

Nancy Z. nodded.

"Are we all squared away now?" Nancy A. held up her blue tote bag and looked at Bea and Paloma again. "You haven't accidentally left anything out of our swag bags, have you?"

Paloma looked appalled.

Nancy A. quickly added, "You know I'm just playing with you. I'm sure you didn't leave out much. Come on, Nancy. Come on, Togo. Let's go see if we can scare up Vic. Or scare a fluffy white cat."

"What was that?" Bea demanded.

"Just complaining about my fiancé's scruffy nightcap," Nancy A. called over her shoulder.

Faith watched the Nancies depart, not sure what to make of them. Then she noticed Bea watching the Nancies too. A furious look flashed in Bea's eyes for just a moment.

Startled, Faith felt a shiver run down her spine.

3

"The two Nancies were baiting us," Paloma said, an indignant tone in her voice. She tore a piece of paper from a notepad and crumpled it into a ball.

"You're right. They were baiting us." Bea turned to Faith, no sign of that disturbing look in her eyes now. "I'm happy to officially meet you."

"It's nice to officially meet you too," Faith replied.

"Thank you for rescuing Snowball," Bea continued. "I should have thanked you immediately, but that situation was so bizarre. I was glad I happened upon you at the right time. For the life of me, I can't remember what I was on my way to do. But everything is fine. Snowball is safe, and that's all that matters."

Faith nodded. "I'm relieved Snowball is all right."

"As for the unfortunate scene you just witnessed," Bea said, "I apologize if it sounded as though things were getting out of hand."

"They're obviously a lively pair," Faith remarked.

"I can think of a less generous description," Bea said, touching her locket. "I appreciate your fresh perspective."

"They didn't even give me a chance to explain," Paloma said. "We tried to book the first weekend in October, because we do like the colloquium to coincide with Edward Stratemeyer's birthday. But Castleton was already booked for that week. We considered going somewhere else—"

"But we always choose venues associated with locations in the original thirty-four Nancy Drew books," Bea interrupted, "and this year we have a triple whammy. Cape Cod is mentioned in *Nancy's Mysterious Letter*, the eighth book. *The Secret of the Wooden Lady*, book twenty-seven, takes place in Boston and Provincetown. And Nancy's boyfriend, Ned Nickerson, attends Emerson College in Boston. So here's this gorgeous manor catering to groups like ours located halfway between Boston and Provincetown at the tip of the Cape. I really don't think that calling it a stunning opportunity is putting it too strongly." She waved her hand dismissively. "Let's forget about the River Heights Roundtable and enjoy ourselves."

"We only hold the colloquium every other year," Paloma went on. "All the arrangements and programming are done by volunteers—a huge amount of work—and if there are more members of the Roundtable registered, they could derail everything. I've seen some of their practical jokes, and I've read online reports about how they've disrupted other conventions."

Faith tried to picture the havoc an unknown number of boisterous Nancy Drew scholars might wreak in the manor. Should she expect a gang of women wearing saddle shoes and carrying magnifying glasses accosting unwary readers and demanding to see their diaries? "Is this an issue our staff should be aware of?" she asked.

"I hardly think so," Bea answered. "As far as I know, Nancy A. and Nancy Z. are the only members of the River Heights Roundtable. At least they're the only ones I've heard of who attend conferences. The group might be more of an online presence." Bea turned to Paloma. "Have you ever heard of them actually being destructive? Or causing property damage?"

"No."

"So then, no, I don't think it will be an issue," Bea said. "We might have gotten off on the wrong foot, and this will certainly be a new experience for me, but maybe we can appeal to their better natures."

"You haven't met them before?" Faith asked.

Bea shook her head.

"I have," Paloma said, "and I think they're nothing but freeloaders. They take advantage of the planning that goes into a conference like this, and they contribute nothing useful in return. They enjoyed making that scene just now. It's how they entertain themselves."

"But if we don't give them the satisfaction of seeing us upset," Bea said, "then they won't win."

"I'll do my best," Paloma promised.

Bea took one of the blue tote bags from the pile next to her on the table and handed it to Faith. "These are the registration bags we're giving to everyone who attends this week. Our program schedule's in it along with a few tchotchkes for fun. I'd like you to have this one, compliments of the Nancy Drew Clue Society."

"Thank you," Faith said, accepting the bag. "That's awfully kind."

"Not at all. Please feel free to sit in on any of our sessions this week. And we'd be delighted if you joined us for dinner this evening. As my way of thanking you for finding and rescuing Snowball."

"I appreciate the invitation," Faith said, "but I have dinner plans with my aunt tonight."

"Change your plans. Invite your aunt too," Bea offered. "We always plan for a few extra seats, so I'll invite Marlene as well. You don't want to miss it. It will be quite a spectacle." She winked at Paloma. "You can see she's tempted, can't you?"

"Aunt Eileen would love it," Faith said. "She's the librarian in Lighthouse Bay and a huge Nancy Drew fan and a mystery fan in general."

"So then it's settled." Bea smiled. "Two librarians will be the perfect addition to the evening."

Faith laughed. "I don't know what to say except thank you. And now I wonder what Aunt Eileen and I will find to wear."

"There's no obligation to dress up," Bea said.

"It would be fun, though," Faith admitted. "What are you wearing?"

"For that, you'll have to wait and see." Bea glanced behind Faith. "Excuse me. There's someone waiting to register."

"Of course. Please be sure to let me know if there's anything I can do for you during your stay at Castleton." Faith turned with a smile for whoever was waiting, but she only saw Lois still at the refreshment table.

Lois raised her teacup.

Faith rejoined her, returning the plate of cookies to where it belonged. "I'm sorry. I didn't mean to make you wait so long to register."

"It didn't bother me," Lois said. "I finished my cup of tea and enjoyed the show. Your intervention by cookie was delightfully Drewian. I hope I'll see you around this week."

"You can count on it."

Eileen Piper, who focused on the positive in most situations, was Faith's aunt. A big part of Faith's joy in taking the job at Castleton Manor was in living so near her mother's sister. Eileen was the head librarian of Lighthouse Bay's privately funded Candle House Library and the leader of the Candle House Book Club. The group had warmly welcomed Faith as a member when she moved to town.

"I really didn't know what to say," Faith told Eileen when she called to tell her about their change in plans.

"Yes was the right answer."

"Absolutely. But I'm not sure I could have gotten away with a no. Bea Stapleton seems decisive and firm."

"To survive and thrive in the ivory tower, you can't be a shrinking violet or a hothouse flower," Eileen said. "What time is dinner?"

"Seven. Cocktails at six."

"Very posh, and that gives me time to ransack my closet—oh! No need to ransack. I know just the thing. For both of us."

"What?" Faith asked.

"I'm not telling. Think of it as a mystery."

"Speaking of which, do you mind doing a bit of sleuthing with me before dinner instead of the cocktails?"

"What are we trying to find out?" Eileen asked.

"I'm not telling."

Watson hadn't reappeared after he followed Marlene from the scene of Snowball's rescue. Faith hadn't had any annoyed phone calls about him from the assistant manager, so she assumed he was entertaining himself without pestering her. She checked each of the chairs in the library and called his name just in case.

When he didn't show his whiskers, she left the room through the French doors and crossed the lawn.

The late-afternoon sun gave the stonework of the cottage a rosy warmth, and Faith stopped to take a picture of it with her phone. She'd sent pictures of the cottage to her grandfather, snapped in every kind of light and weather, and he said he found something new to see in each of them. He was especially good at spotting Watson, even when Faith hadn't realized he was in the shot. Her grandfather liked to say he was putting together a *Where's Watson?* book of the photographs and he expected to find it in the library someday.

As Faith unlocked the front door, the longcase clock in the corner of her living room sounded the half hour. The clock had a mellow tone that Faith thought would be perfect for a signal in a time-travel story.

Tonight she would be swirled back to . . . when? What was Aunt Eileen digging out of a closet or a trunk for them to wear? Something suitable for a ride in a roadster? Something so elegant they could put on airs and call it evening attire?

While she waited to find out, she examined the contents of the conference bag. Bea had been more generous than Faith realized.

In addition to the program brochure, she found two Nancy Drew paperbacks from the series with the most recent incarnation of Nancy, three bookmarks, a Nancy Drew key chain, a mouse pad with a picture of Nancy's blue roadster, a Nancy Drew notepad and pencil, a small magnifying glass, a Nancy Drew cookbook, and an apron celebrating the Stratemeyer Syndicate with a picture of a dapper-looking Edward Stratemeyer and the words *Cooking Up Good Mysteries*.

Faith spread everything out on the kitchen table, and when she heard a car pull up out front, she tied on the apron, picked up the magnifying glass, and went to open the door.

"Don't tell me you've changed your mind about crashing the dinner," Eileen said when she saw the apron.

Faith laughed. "When have you ever known me to pass up free food? I'm just modeling what all the Nancy Drew Clue Colloquium attendees will be wearing in their own kitchens this fall. Do you need help bringing anything in?"

Eileen had a long garment bag draped over her arm and her purse slung over her shoulder. "No. Hands off. You go sit on the sofa, close your eyes, and don't peek."

"You're certainly bossy this evening," Faith complained, but she did as she was told. From her spot on the sofa, she listened to Eileen unzip the garment bag.

"Before I let you look," Eileen said, "did your mother ever show you the old photographs she has of our grandmother?"

"Great-grandmother Florry? A few."

"The one in Boston Public Garden pushing my mother in a baby buggy?"

"Yes, I've always loved that picture. She looked like a movie star in that dress with its cinched waist and puffy sleeves."

"She followed the fashions with her needle and thread. Knitting needles too."

"And you just know she was channeling Katharine Hepburn." Faith opened her eyes. "Oops, sorry. No, not sorry. Where did you get those lovely things?"

"They were Florry's." Eileen smiled as she held up two floor-length evening gowns. "These are for dinner tonight, and when you get home you can see what else is in the bag."

Faith heard a catch of emotion—or excitement—in Eileen's voice, and it gave her an idea of what it might be.

"Now, if we're going to arrive in time for sleuthing before dinner," Eileen said, turning brisk, "we'd better see if these beauties fit. Which one do you want to try on first? Black-and-gold crepe or sapphire silk velvet?"

A whisk of early fall leaves followed Faith and Eileen across the tiled terrace and through the manor's front door into the vestibule.

When they entered the Main Hall, Watson was sitting there, as though waiting for their arrival. He greeted them with the imperturbable blink of a well-trained butler.

"Good evening, Watson," Eileen said. "I believe you're expecting us for dinner and a spot of sleuthing?"

The cat meowed.

Eileen scratched Watson behind the ears, then turned to Faith. "Now tell me what we're up to. Or better yet, tell me what you're getting us into."

Faith looked left, then right, and then behind her to make sure no one was close enough to overhear. "We're investigating the mystery of the haunted staircase," she said quietly.

"The haunted staircase?" Eileen repeated. Then she burst out laughing.

"It does sound absurd when you say it out loud." Faith couldn't help but laugh too.

Marlene strode over to them and cleared her throat. "I'm glad you're finding humor in our small emergency this afternoon."

"I hadn't actually told Aunt Eileen the details," Faith said.

"I was just tickled at the ridiculous idea of anyone thinking the manor is haunted," Eileen replied. "I hope it wasn't anything serious."

"It was aggravating more than serious," Marlene admitted. "Although certainly more serious than funny."

"A cat belonging to a guest got stuck inside one of the hidden passages," Faith explained. "Marlene unlocked the door and let her out."

"After Faith and Watson heard it," Marlene added.

"Thank goodness for all of you," Eileen said. "How did the poor thing get inside the passage?"

"That remains to be seen, but I wouldn't be surprised if Ms. Stapleton's son had something to do with it. And if he's that irresponsible, he might bear watching." Marlene checked her watch. "Now, if you'll excuse me. There's still time for cocktails before dinner."

"Then you go enjoy yourself, and we'll see you in the dining room in a little while." Eileen regarded Marlene's outfit. "By the way, your Nancy Drew costume is spot-on, right down to your saddle shoes."

"You're here for the dinner too?" Marlene looked Faith and Eileen up and down as though she'd just noticed their finery. "You look . . . very nice as well." She sniffed. "I just hope you didn't somehow wheedle your way into an invitation."

Faith smiled and shook her head. When Marlene was gone, she let out a breath.

"If that breath was meant to be a sigh, it sounded more like a growl," Eileen said. "For which you can be forgiven."

"In general, we get along pretty well. Just sometimes . . ." Faith's voice trailed off. Then she told Eileen about the drama surrounding the discovery of Snowball and the disruptions caused by the two Nancies. "I'm pretty sure Bea thinks Snowball was let into the hidden passage on purpose and that she suspects the two Nancies."

"But Marlene thinks it was Bea's son?"

"And I have a different theory." Faith glanced down at her lovely dress. "I promise there will be no traipsing around dusty passages and we won't miss dinner. Are you game?"

Eileen smiled. "Always."

Faith had been in a few of the mansion's hidden passages and knew where some of the secret doors were, including the one that Marlene had opened and one in the library. The passageways had been built for servants to use back in the days when an army of help kept the household running like a well-oiled machine.

Now Faith and Eileen went up the main staircase to the second floor, where the guest suites, a lounge, and a gym were located. The lounge and the gym had windows offering panoramic views of the ocean. Guests were also able to access the library from the second floor.

"What are we searching for?" Eileen asked.

"I know there's a hidden door in one of the storerooms. Maybe that hidden door was opened and left open, and Snowball got in that way. But there must be other ways in and out of the passages. That's the only explanation for how Watson gets around sometimes."

"Have you ever asked him how he does it?" Eileen said.

"I've followed him up here a few times," Faith admitted. "But every time I think I'm being stealthy, he turns around and looks at me. And if he isn't making it into a game, then he knows how to shake me. He'll go around a corner, and just like that, I've lost him."

"So what do you suspect?"

"I'm wondering if there might be cat-size openings in some of the closets and storage areas for ventilation in the passages."

Eileen raised her eyebrows. "That makes very good sense."

When they reached the second floor, Faith led Eileen down a wide corridor. The deep carpet in the corridor hushed their footsteps. The guest rooms were not numbered. Instead, they were named after beloved authors. They passed the Charles Dickens Suite and the Arthur Conan Doyle Suite.

Faith stopped. "If any openings exist, they're probably meant to have screens or grates over them."

"In case of varmints?"

Faith grinned. "Like debonair cats in fur tuxedos."

"If you're right," Eileen said, "then some of the grates could be missing. And if the opening is in a closet or a storeroom, a missing grate might not be noticed."

"Exactly," Faith said. "The times I've trailed Watson up here, I've lost him around this next corner. One time the storeroom door was open, but when I went in, the hidden door was shut. I even wondered if Watson somehow discovered a pressure-sensitive mechanism for getting in and out."

"That would be ingenious."

"And more complicated than vents so the servants didn't suffocate. Up until now, I've been looking for doors in front of me, not for air vents near the ceiling. Come on. Let's take a look."

Faith started around the corner, but she hastily stepped back again, turning her head so Eileen could see the finger to her lips. She stopped where she could peek around the corner without being seen. She hoped.

A young man stood at the door to one of the suites, his back to her, his head inclined as though listening for something behind the door. He tentatively reached a hand toward the doorknob, but he didn't touch it.

The word *skulking* popped into Faith's head. She turned again to Eileen and whispered, "Follow my lead."

Then she stepped briskly around the corner, ready to smile and ask the young man how she could help, only to find the corridor completely empty.

"He pulled a Watson," Eileen concluded when Faith told her how the young man she'd spotted in the corridor had disappeared. "Do you have any idea who he was?"

Faith frowned. "I only saw the back of his head. It might have been Bea's son, but I can't be sure. This guy seemed taller and slimmer, but that's only an impression. That he was skulking is only an impression too."

"What was he wearing?" her aunt persisted.

"Good point," Faith said. "If I can remember. A tweed jacket, I think. It looked slightly large."

"That might help identify him."

"If he doesn't change or leave. Oh, two more things." Faith went to the storeroom door but found it locked. Then she crossed the hall and read the suite's nameplate. She didn't react until she rejoined Eileen, and then she laughed softly. "Guess which suite it is."

Eileen studied Faith's face, thought for a moment, and then she laughed too. "It has to be the Nancy Drew Suite."

"Yes indeed. And if we ask, I think we'll hear that Bea is staying in the Nancy Drew Suite, which makes me even more curious about what the mysterious man in the hallway was up to."

Eileen put her arm through Faith's. "Then let us proceed to the banquet hall, Lady Faith, and if we don't find answers, we can at least seek further adventures."

The banquet hall was immense and sumptuous with a huge fireplace at one end and six freestanding gold alabaster columns along each side. The columns supported a swag-enriched frieze and cornice.

Faith and Eileen slipped into the room shortly before the guests arrived from the cocktail party being held in the Great Hall Gallery.

Eileen tipped her head back and gazed at the vaulted ceiling soaring above them. "Such an amazing room. I love how you can see the French influence in the details of the stonework."

"In the fabrics too," Faith said. "And that seems appropriate tonight, because I feel a bit like Cinderella."

"You look lovely—as though you stepped out of a photograph taken in this room eighty years ago."

"Except for our hairstyles, we both look like we belong here."

"In our own miniscule way," Eileen said, "but this place needs at least two dozen people in evening wear to do it justice. You and I are swallowed up. Surely when Charlotte and Henry were raising the boys in the manor, they didn't use this as their dining room."

"Three boys running around anywhere in the manor boggles your mind, doesn't it? Wolfe and his brothers must have had their supper in the more human-size dining room on the third floor. I wonder if they ever ate tomato soup from a can or mac and cheese from a box?"

Eileen laughed.

When the guests started to trickle into the banquet hall, Eileen whispered, "When you see the two Nancies, will you point them out to me?"

"Of course." Faith heard snatches of conversation about powdering noses and saving seats, but the slow arrival made it easier to see and admire the clothes.

Most of the guests were middle-aged women, a handful appeared to be in their twenties, and a few were in their seventies or above. Lois, whom Faith guessed to be in her early eighties, came in pushing the wheelchair of a woman who looked as though she might have read the earlier Nancy Drew books when they were a brand-new sensation.

"Do you see the mystery man?" Eileen discreetly gestured to two men. "What about one of them?"

Faith shook her head. Neither was slim enough to be the man in the corridor.

"Look at that woman in the black-and-red gown," Eileen commented. "Doesn't she look like a femme fatale?"

"The next one is brave. Her gown is backless."

Eileen shivered. "She makes me very glad for the warmth of this velvet."

"Here you go," Faith said. "See the chartreuse green? That's Nancy Z., and Nancy A. is behind her in the leather jacket. The guy is Vic, Nancy A.'s fiancé. You know, this might show the limits of my imagination, but I've never thought of Nancy Drew as a punk rocker."

"But she somehow makes it work. The fake nail through her nose is an interesting touch." Eileen paused. "It *is* fake, isn't it?"

In addition to the nail through her nose, Nancy A. wore a black leather letter jacket with the letters *ND* in the middle of her chest, a red plaid mini kilt, tattered fishnet stockings, and black boots that laced to her knees.

Nancy Z. clashed with her cohort dramatically. She wore a tight chartreuse-green satin gown that flared out below her knees and swept the floor, giving the impression of a mermaid's tail. The flounced tier of ruffles at the shoulders would have been demure on a lesser gown.

The trio spotted Faith and Eileen and made a beeline for them.

"Hi, I'm Vic. My name's not important, though, so long as you know I'm with these two." He motioned to the Nancies. "So who are you? The bouncers for this shindig?"

Nancy A. swatted Vic's shoulder and then readjusted the nail that was clipped to her nose. "I told you. Bea and Paloma are in charge. This is the librarian who came to the rescue with a plate of cookies this afternoon, just like Hannah would have done."

"Who's Hannah?" Vic asked.

"Quiet," the Nancies said in unison.

"Hannah Gruen is Nancy Drew's housekeeper," Faith said, taking pity on Vic, who was rubbing his shoulder after another swat from Nancy A. "I'm Faith Newberry. We met in the lobby this afternoon."

"And I'm Eileen, Faith's aunt and happy hanger-on for the evening."

"Pleased to meet you," Vic said. "I bet you know who these two are already." He'd wisely moved out of easy reach of Nancy A., and after offering that observation, he became more interested in taking in the banquet hall than in further conversation.

"Vic!" Nancy A. called as he wandered off.

"Let him go. He'll find us when we sit down," Nancy Z. said, then turned to Faith and Eileen. "So, where are you two sitting? Why don't you join us at our table?"

Faith and Eileen glanced at each other.

"Ah. Got it." Nancy A. nodded. "You're with the bee and the bird."

"Sorry?" Faith asked.

"Bea and Paloma," Nancy Z. clarified. "*Paloma* is 'dove' in Spanish, so the bee and the bird."

"Thank you for asking. We'd otherwise love to sit with you, but Bea did ask us first." Faith scanned the room. "I wonder where they are."

"If they see you with us, they won't be coming over to chat," Nancy A. said. "They avoided us at the cocktail party."

"And if we're lucky, they'll avoid us in here too," Nancy Z. added.

"Are they really so bad?" Eileen asked. "I haven't met Bea, but—oh, the cat." She glanced at Faith. "I hope nothing else mysterious has happened to her."

Faith watched the Nancies. She didn't consider herself an expert in reading faces, but she only saw mild interest and curiosity, nothing like conspiracy or guilt.

"Going by first impressions only, wouldn't you guess that Bea's a cat person?" Nancy A. remarked. Before anyone could answer, she continued, "So what mysterious thing happened to her cat?"

Faith turned to Nancy Z. "I hate to spoil your fun over the haunted staircase."

"The cat?" Nancy Z. said. "The ghost was Bea's *cat*?"

"Who, what, where, when, and how?" Nancy A. asked. "You must tell me all, and then I cannot possibly ever let Bea live it down."

"Do you really think—" Faith started to say.

"But I know what it's like to worry about a pet," Nancy A. interrupted. "I'll wait until the colloquium is over, and *then* I won't let Bea live it down. Now, before the bee and the bird show up, we'll get lost so we don't taint you with our presence."

The Nancies both laughed, then made their raucous way to the other end of the room.

"When you take in the architecture, the decor, and the vast scale of this room," Eileen said, "there's already a lot of drama going on. But bring in several dozen people fanatic about a fictional character and throw a couple of real characters like the Nancies into the mix?"

"Too much?" Faith asked.

"I wouldn't have missed it for the world." Eileen's eyes sparkled. "And if I'm not mistaken, here come the bee and the bird."

"Let's not call them that," Faith said. "Please?"

"Nothing shall pass my lips that any librarian will ever feel the need to hush."

They watched as Bea and Paloma entered the banquet hall and greeted some of the guests milling around. Bea looked regal in a gown with waves of feathery white ruffles at her neckline and floating around her shoulders. From her shoulders down, the gown was beaded white satin.

"Bea's dress must weigh a ton," Faith said.

Eileen nodded. "And it didn't come from a costume shop. It's as real as yours and mine. It looks Hollywood red carpet all the way. I didn't think it was possible, but now I feel dumpy and dowdy in my sapphire velvet."

"Paloma might be feeling the same way," Faith commented, "and there's nothing wrong with her dress at all."

Paloma's black dress appeared several decades younger than Bea's. It was fitted through the bodice, and the calf-length skirt flared from a stiff petticoat that was visible when she made quick movements. It was elegant and classic, and it appeared as plain and unnoticeable as a poor relation next to Bea's glamour.

Only Lois and her friend were already seated at one of the tables. The rest of the guests were apparently waiting for Bea's signal. Faith hadn't seen names at the place settings, and she assumed from Nancy Z.'s invitation to sit with them that choosing seats was more or less a polite free-for-all.

Now Faith noticed people approaching the tables, not quite jockeying for position but making it clear the general area they'd like to sit. So it surprised her to see Paloma cutting in front of people at the end of the table nearest to them and putting *Reserved* cards at the first three places down either side. She heard only one grumble as people moved away.

Paloma waved Faith over. "Bea asked me to make sure you and your aunt sit with us." She turned to Eileen. "Hello, I'm Paloma Martin."

"Eileen Piper. It's very kind of you to include me."

"We're delighted to have you. Faith, sit here on the end. You'll be across from Bea. Eileen, you're between me and Faith. Of course you know Marlene, across from you, and on her right is Drew."

"Pleased to meet you," Drew said. He smiled at Marlene, Faith, and Eileen, and he continued to smile as he looked down the length of the table, at the ceiling, and then down to the plate in front of him. The same vacant smile for all.

Faith watched Bea's son, trying not to be obvious about it. A sideways glance at Eileen showed that she was doing the same.

When Drew started to reach for his glass of water, hesitated, and apparently decided against it, she felt Eileen's foot touch hers and knew her aunt was wondering if Drew could be the mystery man.

"Faith, dear," Eileen said, again touching her foot to Faith's, "did you ever remember the punch line to that joke you were going to tell me?"

"Sorry, no. I'll keep trying, though." As coded communication, Faith thought Eileen's effort was as good as anything Nancy Drew ever used.

"What joke?" Marlene asked.

Instantly, every joke flew out of Faith's head that didn't have a punch line so obvious there was no way she could have forgotten it.

Luckily, at that moment Bea arrived at the head of the table in all her white satin and ruffled glory and called the room to order. "Welcome, everyone, to this year's Nancy Drew Clue Colloquium. For those of you who don't know me, I'm Bea Stapleton, president of the Nancy Drew Clue Society, the group that convenes the colloquium semiannually."

The audience clapped.

"We have six full days of discussions and activities planned for you," Bea announced, "including a trivia game and craft session, both of which are open to the public. And rides are being offered in some of the remarkable vintage cars."

There was another round of applause.

Bea smiled. "Finally, we have an exciting addition to the schedule that's so new it didn't even make it into the program. We're delighted to provide tours of the hidden passages here in Castleton Manor."

Guests oohed and aahed.

Faith hadn't heard about the tours, but when she glanced at Marlene, she didn't seem the least bit surprised.

"In all sincerity I'd like to say that the presence of every one of you will make this the best colloquium we've had to date," Bea continued. "And now, enjoy your dinner. From the menu cards at your places, you'll see that it's a meal Hannah Gruen would be proud to serve."

The group laughed and applauded.

Bea sat down and warmly greeted Faith and Eileen, her silver locket glinting like a brilliant shard from one of the crystal chandeliers overhead.

"That's beautiful," Faith said, touching her own throat, as though feeling the necklace there. "I've never seen a broken-heart locket quite like that. If you don't mind my asking, does someone wear the other half?"

"Thank you," Bea said. "But I prefer not to talk about it. I'm sorry."

"Forgive me for asking." Faith felt a twinge of guilt for inadvertently bringing up a sensitive subject.

Bea turned to Marlene, but she seemed to have some trouble seeing the assistant manager over her ruffled shoulder. She compacted the ruffles a bit, only to find Marlene's back to her as she conversed with Drew. "It's my son's first colloquium," Bea said to the others, letting the ruffles revive. "I'm glad to see he's already enjoying himself."

Faith thought Bea might not sound so optimistic if she had a view of her son unencumbered by feathered ruffles and Marlene. From where Faith sat he looked stoic at best. But despite Drew's earlier vacant smile and his current aloof demeanor, Faith thought she detected humor and forbearance too. She imagined he'd needed both as a boy named Drew who was the son of a Nancy Drew scholar.

Waitstaff brought the first course—Double Jinx Salad according to Faith's menu card—which turned out to be a poached pear half that was filled with curried pecans, cranberries, and crumbles of blue cheese on a bed of greens.

"There's no way Hannah Gruen was serving curried pecans and blue cheese in River Heights in the 1930s," Drew said.

Faith was about to agree when Marlene beat her to it.

"In fact," Marlene said, "the original recipe called for the pear to be filled with a mixture of mayonnaise, cottage cheese, and a few drops of green food coloring. All of that held two pear halves together. You're meant to stand the pear up on the lettuce leaves and stick a green olive on top—as a stem, I suppose. I think our kitchen staff improved on that by quite a bit."

Drew took another bite, then nodded enthusiastically. He pulled his menu card from under the salad plate and read aloud, "'Crooked

Bannister Corn Bread, The Case of the Smothered Pork Chops, The Cousins' Special Cauliflower, and Twisted Candles Peach Crisp.' The possibility for an atrocious meal is staring me right in the face."

"Utterly," Marlene said. "The names are straight out of *The Nancy Drew Cookbook*, and anything that has to be smothered in order to be edible is automatically suspect, but judging by this salad, we can put our trust in the staff."

Faith decided it was safe to say that at this point, Drew *was* enjoying himself. So was Marlene, and that was nice to see.

"Faith told me about the unusual adventure your cat had this afternoon," Eileen said to Bea.

"Unusual to say the least," Bea replied. "It was Marlene's generous suggestion to offer tours of the hidden passages as a way to make up for the incident. Not that I blame Castleton staff for what happened."

"I'm sure Snowball is happy to be back in your suite," Faith said. "You're in the Nancy Drew, aren't you?"

"Yes, and it's a lovely room." Bea smiled. "Snowball was napping on the chaise like a pampered princess when I came downstairs for cocktails."

"This afternoon you told me that you thought you knew what happened," Faith reminded her. "And I appreciate and respect what you said about not spreading rumors. Are you still satisfied with what you suspected earlier?"

"Ah. Well, it's possible I was hasty in assigning blame." Bea patted down a few of the ruffles around her neck. "I almost feel as though I owe Nancy A. and Nancy Z. an apology for thinking they had something to do with it."

Paloma made a noise of protest.

Bea shook her head. "You didn't hear the awful things I said in the privacy of my suite, Paloma. But then, neither did the Nancies, hence the 'almost' about owing them an apology. Instead, I made a point of sounding as inclusive as I could in my welcome, and I'll leave it at that."

"You did that very nicely," Eileen assured her. "What changed your mind about the Nancies and Snowball?"

"A private discussion," Bea said. "Are you at all crafty? Because we'd love to have you join us for crafts and coffee on Thursday morning."

Faith admired Bea's smooth transition to the safer topic of knitting needles and glue guns. She'd also noticed a very slight hesitation over the phrase "private discussion." As though Bea had reached for another phrase but thought better of it. Like Drew and his water glass. Or the young man in the corridor. All three hesitating over something.

What had Marlene said about smothering? *Anything that has to be smothered to be edible is automatically suspect.* So what was Bea's private discussion smothering?

And why am I looking for mysteries to solve around every corner? It must be my inner Nancy Drew, desperate to get out. Have I been smothering her for too long?

Faith almost laughed at the thought, and when she saw Drew watching her, she wondered if she had. She smiled, and he looked away.

Then she caught movement in the corner of her eye. She turned to see someone getting up from a nearby table.

A young man in a tweed jacket bent to hear something the woman seated next to him said. A moment later he put his napkin on the back of his chair and headed out the banquet hall door.

5

Faith considered hopping up and going after the mystery man. *But to do what?* By the time she decided to ask Bea who the young man was, he was already gone.

She decided it wouldn't hurt to ask about him anyway. "Excuse me, Bea. One of the guests is a young man about Drew's age. I thought I recognized him, but I'm not sure why."

"The mystery of the disappearing man?" Eileen asked.

"That's it exactly," Faith said. "Not to mention the disappearing memory. I can't dredge up a name."

"I can solve it for you," Paloma offered. "We don't have many men in the group, and Ned Carson is the only one close to Drew's age. So you know Ned? He's a graduate student in Boston."

"The name doesn't ring a bell, but we might have crossed paths in Boston. I used to be an academic librarian there." And they might have crossed paths, Faith realized, although knowing that didn't tell her any more about Ned Carson. "Thank you. At least now I won't be racking my brain for a name or hunting him down to stare at him."

"I certainly hope you don't hunt guests down and stare at them," Marlene chimed in.

Drew snorted, which made Marlene snort.

Faith told Eileen she'd be right back, excused herself, and went to say hello to Lois.

Lois took Faith's hand in both of hers. "You look stunning, my dear." She glanced at the head table and asked, "What are Bea and your friend Marlene going to do?"

Bea raised a hand above her sea of ruffles and called for the guests' attention.

Marlene, looking like Watson when he'd scored an extra treat, stood next to her.

"Before our main course is served," Bea said, "Marlene Russell, Castleton Manor's assistant manager, has an announcement." She gestured to Marlene and sat down.

Marlene held up an envelope but didn't say anything. Faith knew that Marlene didn't like speaking in public, and she wondered if she'd frozen. But she didn't look tense or nervous. She still looked smug.

Some of the guests gave each other uneasy glances. People whispered, and then someone at the far end of the table made a *ticktock* noise.

One of the Nancies? Faith looked over.

Nancy Z. saw her and wiggled her fingers in a wave.

"I'm sorry to drop a mystery into your laps this evening," Marlene finally said. "But I received a letter earlier this afternoon, and I don't know who sent it to me."

Faith glanced around the room and saw only rapt attention from the audience, even from the Nancies.

"This letter is a mystery," Marlene stated, "and I believe it concerns all of us because it indicates that a friend of ours might be in peril." She paused. "I hope that what I'm about to read doesn't cast a pall over the colloquium."

A male voice from the far end of the table called out, "You're killing us with suspense!"

Faith turned in time to see Nancy A. swat Vic on the shoulder.

"I haven't opened the envelope yet," Marlene continued, "and I hope there's no need to. You see, there's a note on the envelope that says, 'This is my insurance. In the event of my death, please open.' The note is signed 'Nancy.'"

Faith turned again. This time she saw Nancy A.'s face go slack, then twist with an emotion Faith couldn't identify. *Fear? Fury?*

Marlene scanned the audience. "As I said, it's a mystery, and I fear it means you should be prepared for more mysteries to come."

Nancy A. jumped to her feet and rushed out of the room.

Faith waited to see if Vic or Nancy Z. would go after her.

When neither of them did, she went. But it obviously wasn't her day for catching up to people. By the time she got to the door, Nancy A. was out of sight. She heard footsteps and tried to follow them, but with the marble floors, connecting corridors, and spaces open to the second floor with more corridors, she soon lost the footsteps in a maze of echoes.

Feeling defeated, Faith stood in the corridor and wondered about Nancy A.'s reaction to the mysterious letter.

Then a voice pulled her out of her thoughts. "Are you looking for something?"

She turned and saw Ned Carson. "I didn't hear you coming."

"Sorry. I didn't mean to startle you. I'm light on my feet, and I'm wearing crepe soles. I can show you the way to the banquet hall, if that's where you're going." Ned inclined his head in that direction, and they started walking. "It isn't far."

"And I'm not really lost," Faith admitted.

"Oh, good. That's an excellent quality in anyone."

"I'm the librarian here at Castleton. Faith Newberry."

"I know," he said.

When they reached the banquet hall, Ned lifted a hand in something that wasn't quite a wave and left Faith standing and staring after him.

"I thought you weren't going to stare when you found him," Eileen teased when Faith reclaimed her seat.

"I can't believe you saw that," Faith said with a laugh.

"So what was he like?" Eileen asked.

"Unknown quantity sums it up," Faith answered.

"Great job on the letter," Bea said to Marlene. "It was very dramatic."

"Thank you. It was a bit of fun. I was glad to help out."

"We haven't done something like this before," Bea said. "We're always looking for suggestions and new activities to spice things up, and receiving a mysterious letter set the tone beautifully."

Marlene furrowed her brow but remained silent.

"I loved the way you built up the suspense, Marlene," Paloma added, "and I can't wait for more. If you'll let us know when you're ready to spring the next surprise, we'll adjust the schedule to account for audience reaction if we need to."

"Yes, I'm sorry we didn't let you in on it tonight," Bea told Paloma. "When Marlene approached me, there wasn't much time, and I went on gut instinct."

Faith noticed that Marlene's furrow had deepened. Something wasn't quite right. "Where did the letter come from?" she asked.

"From Marlene," Bea said promptly. "This was her fantastic idea."

"Is this part of the play?" Drew asked. "Because I'm really getting into it."

"Wonderful!" Bea clapped. "Didn't I say that Castleton Manor is the perfect place for the colloquium?"

One of the guests approached the table and whispered to Bea and Paloma, then whisked them away.

When they were gone, Marlene shook her head. "The letter wasn't my idea," she said quietly. "It was delivered to my office this afternoon. It seemed clear it was meant to be part of the staging for the week. To add atmosphere."

"Where is it now?" Faith asked.

"Right here." Marlene picked up the sealed envelope from the table.

"Did you open it?" Faith persisted.

"Of course not. I was waiting for further instructions." Marlene hesitated. "Should we open it?"

"I think we should put it in the safe," Faith replied.

Marlene studied the envelope, dropped it on the table, and scrubbed her fingers with her napkin. "What *does* happen next?"

"I think we'll have to wait and see," Eileen said.

While the humans enjoyed their noisy party with no regard to the safety of their perimeter or the handing of tidbits to hungry heroes, the cat sacrificed much-needed nap time to patrolling the corridors of the manor.

The cat pondered the current ratio of visiting canines to felines. It could hardly be more lopsided, offering further proof of the superiority of feline intelligence and honor. Most cats had obviously elected to stay home and remain on duty while the dogs and their humans came here to frolic and be pampered.

On this night, no dogs were loose. No ungrateful, heroically rescued creatures stirred. All would be quiet, except for the loud voices behind the door where one of the dogs was whining. Angry, shouting voices made the cat's whiskers and ears twitch the way he remembered his kitten tail twitching to warn him of danger. Only once had he ignored his tail. That had been a hard lesson to learn.

He had since heard it said that a cat without a tail is like a ship without a rudder. He took exception to that view, but then again, he was exceptional. He had also heard that which does not kill you makes you stronger. He preferred this saying because he was living proof of its truth.

The cat listened to the angry voices until his ears and whiskers had had too much. Then he steered himself, with exceptional grace and exactitude, to the spiral steps that allowed him to descend into his human's book-lined lair—a place where cats and their ears and whiskers could dream in peace.

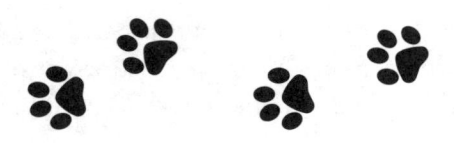

"There you are, Watson," Faith said.

After dinner, Faith and Eileen searched for the cat and found him asleep on one of the chairs in the library.

"Ready to go?" Faith scooped Watson into her arms. "He must be exhausted because usually he doesn't let me carry him home," she said to Eileen. "We'll go out the French doors. It'll be quicker."

Light from the manor spilled from the windows, illuminating some of the way home to the cottage. A full moon overhead did the rest.

"You aren't the only one who had a long day, Rumpy," Faith said, using her nickname for him. She rubbed her cheek against the top of his head as they walked. "Poor Marlene. I won't be surprised if she doesn't sleep at all."

"Do you think she can withstand the temptation to open that letter?" Eileen asked.

Faith stopped when they approached the cottage. "I believe she can. She's tough. But I wonder how she'll handle the situation with Bea and Paloma. They think she's planned more mysterious surprises."

"Maybe she'll ask you to help her come up with a few," Eileen suggested as she unlocked her car. "That might be amusing."

"It might be." Faith hugged her aunt good night and watched her drive away.

It wasn't until she went inside that she realized she hadn't thanked Eileen again for the dress—and the garment bag still draped across the chair in the living room. She nestled Watson in the other chair.

The cat was immediately wide awake. He hopped down and went straight to the kitchen.

"Bring me a cup of tea while you're out there, will you?" Faith called after him.

She went to her bedroom and changed out of the evening gown into comfortable sweats. Then she returned to the living room, took a breath, and felt the tingle in her fingers as she unzipped the garment bag. Inside were two more hangers, but the garments on each were shrouded in muslin. *The ghosts of Great-Grandmother Florry past.*

She removed the first hanger from the bag and unveiled it, revealing a pair of wool trousers. She took them off the hanger and held them up—wide-legged trousers. They were the high-waisted kind she'd seen Katharine Hepburn wearing in movies from the thirties. *They're very cool but not what I expected . . .*

She took the second hanger from the bag. It was tempting to fling the muslin off in one go, but she called on every ounce of self-discipline and took the muslin off with respect for Florry and the garment inside.

Watson came back from the kitchen in time to witness the reveal.

Faith put a hand to her heart. "This is it, Watson. The dress my great-grandmother wore in the picture." She wondered if it was weird to suddenly feel as though the young Florry who'd worn this dress now stood in the room with her.

She held up the dress and gasped. "I had no idea it was red and white. Or that it was so beautiful."

The dress was made of red batiste covered in large, overlapping white polka dots. It had a red sash and the short tails of a matching tie at the neck. A seam below the bust accentuated the length and shape of the dress. What looked like short dolman sleeves was a double layer of loose ruffles. A wide Peter Pan collar gave the appearance of a third layer on the shoulders.

Faith carried the dress to the bedroom and put it on. After a twirl in front of the mirror, she called Eileen. "I'm sorry. I didn't even think about the time. Were you asleep?"

"No, because I knew you'd call."

"Where were these clothes? Where did you find them?"

"In a wardrobe in Mom and Dad's attic. Did you ever go up there?"

"They wouldn't let us. I was afraid to anyway, and Jenna was terrified. Of course that might have had something to do with her fear of spiders and my story about the whole attic being filled with one humongous spiderweb." Faith chuckled. "I think I believed that story too, and it served me right for scaring her."

"To be fair, there *were* spiders up there," Eileen said, "and it was dusty, but they really didn't keep much up there. That's why I was so surprised when Dad brought these clothes down. They'd hung in the wardrobe for decades, covered with cotton bedsheets to keep them clean. Your mother wasn't interested, so I took them. Florry made the red one herself. I have some of her patterns too. I thought I'd do a display at the library."

"Do you want the dresses and trousers for it?"

"No, they're yours now, if you want them. The red-and-white one is an afternoon dress. From the way the gown fit, I'd say the red one will fit you perfectly."

"It does. I'm just wondering if I dare wear it."

"Katharine Hepburn would wear it while she searched for a leopard with Cary Grant."

"No leopards around here—hey! Sorry, Aunt Eileen. The 'hey' was for Watson. He just walked past and swatted my ankle."

"You insulted his leopardhood. But we're on the wrong track with Hepburn and Grant. As Paloma would say, get your Nancy Drew on. You've got clues to follow."

The cat knew he had clues to follow and questions to answer. He also knew his human would fret if he asked to go out and didn't return in "two shakes of Rumpy's stumpy tail," a joke she'd made up and thought he enjoyed as much as she did.

When his human agreed to open the door for him, he let her know, with a slow blink, that he would be happy to wake her from the deepest sleep to let him back in.

The night smelled of swooping owls and mice that did not dally.

The cat did not dally either. He knew a secret way into the manor and made silent and stealthy work of slinking up to the second floor, where he lifted his nose. When the angry voices had interrupted him earlier, he had just caught an interesting whiff. And there it was again—a scent that scurried and hid. Creeping low to the floor, he followed it around a corner.

Only to be vexed by another interruption. A human, looking left and right, stopped and crouched outside a door, phone in hand. A finger flicked, and insistent tapping danced from the phone, like so many careless feet, sending the cat streaking back into the night and home.

6

Faith and Watson left for work together the next morning.

"Are you feeling all right?" she asked him. "You seem preoccupied."

He'd let half a dozen dry leaves scud past him without a single pounce, and a grasshopper jumping to get away from her feet hadn't even caught his attention.

"You were sneezing yesterday. Maybe I'd better see if Midge is in the clinic this morning and take you in."

Watson first danced sideways, his stub of a tail puffed into a brief exclamation point, then leaped straight up into the air and raced off.

Faith laughed. "You don't need to run away just because I mentioned the vet."

She caught up to him on the terrace at the door to the library.

Watson flicked his front paws and then licked them. When she unlocked the door, he sauntered through, nose in the air.

"You're a complete and utter goofball," Faith said as she followed him inside.

"That's a fine way to greet your employer." Wolfe Jaxon straightened from bending over a display case near Faith's desk.

Watson showed no signs of being surprised to find Wolfe in the library.

But Faith, not expecting anyone in the room she knew she'd locked before leaving, barely kept herself from uttering a startled response. Of course, as co-owner of Castleton Manor, Wolfe had keys and access to everything.

She caught her breath and smiled. "Welcome back. How was Chicago?"

"Beautiful lakefront. Fabulous pizza. Great hot dogs. Wonderful exhibit at the Art Institute."

"You make it sound awfully hard to leave."

Wolfe shrugged. "I didn't see any of it. I was stuck in meetings the whole time, and for all the progress we made, I might as well have conducted business over the phone from here." He put a hand to the middle of his back. "And that boardroom needs better chairs. Sorry. I shouldn't complain."

"Don't worry about it. I won't tell Chicago."

"That's not what I'm worried about," Wolfe said, then looked again at the display Faith had put together.

She'd chosen photos, diaries, letters, and memorabilia from the library archives to give the colloquium guests a glimpse of life at Castleton Manor and on Cape Cod in the early 1930s when the first Nancy Drew books were published.

Faith had enjoyed writing captions and a few longer labels to better explain the context of some of the material that included several period photos of the Jaxon family and a child's drawing of the mansion's floor plan, complete with arrows and faded red *X*'s marking hidden doors and passages.

When she'd gathered the pieces, she hadn't thought any of them were too personal, but now she wondered. "No? So what are you worried about?"

"Why exactly did you call me a complete and utter goofball?"

The cat was not always able to tell the difference between a human attempting humor and a human about to become hysterical. It was a fine and possibly flexible line to judge, even when it came to his human, with whom he felt exceptionally simpatico. She was one of the least hysterical humans he had encountered. This was mainly because he had taken it upon himself to instruct her in the ways of feline purification—or

purr-ification (a small joke he enjoyed because its clarity and cleverness so subtly illustrated his own sense of humor).

Another unhysterical human, who had recently come into the cat's sphere of knowledge, was the nice man.

The nice man had just asked a question that must have made little sense.

Why else would it give his human pause?

Faith hesitated after Wolfe's question. *Does he really think that I was talking to him when I called Watson a goofball?* But no, she saw the twitch of a smile.

And then Watson launched himself from her desk onto the display case between them, rolled onto his side, and batted Wolfe's hand playfully with his soft paws.

"Here's the goofball." Faith laughed. "Complete and utter. Watson, what are you doing?"

Wolfe rubbed Watson between the ears. He was rewarded with a deep purr. "May I say your basso profundo is a fine choice today, sir? Do remember you're in a library, though, and keep the rumbles to a reasonable level."

Watson continued purring.

Wolfe looked at Faith. "He's a fine fellow and as handsome as my forebears in the photographs in your display here. Nice job. I'd forgotten about the map, and I'm glad to see it again."

"I love it. It's a gem."

"The job here is still going well?"

Faith nodded. "I love it too."

"That's great to hear." Wolfe smiled. "I'll be working from Castleton all this week. I'm sure I'll see you around."

Faith watched Wolfe thread his way between the leather wingback chairs as he headed to the door. *He's as graceful as Watson. That is, when Watson isn't being a goofball.*

She was glad that Wolfe's question about her job had been so easy to answer. She did love it. She often found herself thinking of the library as her sanctuary, but in truth, she rarely needed a place of sanctuary at the manor. The booklovers who came to stay for a few nights or a few weeks helped to create an atmosphere she thrived on—a curious mix of inspiration, imagination, lively discussion, and serenity.

It's a bookish atmosphere, and the manor is steeped in it. It just happens to be strongest in the library. As it should be.

As remarkable as the rest of Castleton Manor was, the room that most impressed guests was the library. It was a hushed, walnut-paneled marvel of books, from the floor to the frescoed ceiling two stories above.

If the library had been available to guests twenty-four hours a day, Faith felt sure some of them would never leave—as evidenced by the way she had to gently encourage them out the door before she locked up for the day. She had visions of arriving some morning and finding a guest or two camped out under a table or snuggled with a pillow in one of the wingback chairs.

Faith was often asked to contribute her expertise in one way or another to seminars and retreats held at the manor. The Nancy Drew Clue Society had made all the arrangements themselves, so she planned to work on a huge project she'd been itching to get into—better organization and cataloging of the archive collections. She wouldn't finish the task this week or even this month, but she was eager to map out a plan and begin. And this seemed like the ideal time.

If she had been superstitious or feeling more fanciful than usual, she might have thought Watson had just rolled his eyes as though to say, "Famous last words." But she wasn't either of those two things, so she sat down at her desk and opened her laptop.

As soon as she created a new document, Watson hopped down

from the display case and went to greet their first visitors—Marlene and Lois.

Lois said hello to Watson and thanked Marlene for helping her find her way, and then she only had eyes for the library.

"For most of my adult life I've dreamed of spending a vacation in a beautiful room like this," Lois murmured. "I never thought I'd actually get the chance, but this is everything I hoped it would be. I almost wouldn't need food or water. I could live here on air and books."

"If you do require anything else during your stay," Marlene said, "we'll be happy to supply it."

Lois slowly wandered off, gazing around the room, her expression reflecting a state of total awe and bliss.

Marlene went over to Faith. "I wonder if you can give me a hand with something," she said without preamble.

"Of course. What can I do for you?"

"It concerns these tours of the passageways," Marlene replied.

"Oh yes, I was wondering about the arrangements for them."

"Good. I'm glad we're on the same wavelength, so then you won't mind working up a spiel. You know, a few stories and interesting tidbits. I'm sure you'll find plenty of material in the archives. Let's plan on no more than twenty minutes, and be sure to allow some time for a few questions. Consider it more of an entertaining jaunt than a hike."

"Who's going to lead the tours?" Faith asked, even though she had a feeling she already knew the answer.

"If we each take two of them, our regular work won't be quite so disrupted. But I might have to let you take three because I have a prior commitment. Laura can be here and free you up."

Laura was a young woman who worked in housekeeping and occasionally for Faith in the library. Her help in the library was invaluable, giving Faith's own schedule more flexibility, but Laura was also a hardworking student.

"She's been so busy with classes lately," Faith said. "Are you sure—"

"I already checked," Marlene interrupted. "Laura doesn't have any classes this afternoon, and I rearranged her housekeeping schedule."

"It sounds like it's a plan. Do you have a route in mind?"

"Will knowing the route make a difference?" Marlene asked.

"It might help for writing the script."

"*Script.* That's the word I was looking for. See? You're just the person to write it. I'll e-mail the route to you."

"When—"

"The first tour leaves the library at three," Marlene interrupted again. "Thank you for pitching in. You take the first three tours, and I should be back in time to take the last one. If you keep people moving along, the whole thing should be over in no more than two hours."

"Do you mean three o'clock this afternoon?" Faith asked.

"Of course." Marlene turned and strode out of the library.

Faith sighed. She wished she could take a brisk walk outside to work off steam, but then she'd have to lock the library. Lois and now another guest were happily browsing, so Faith settled for deep breaths.

Then Laura came in.

Wafted in, Faith thought. *She really isn't much wider than a cat whisker.*

"I'm sorry we disrupted your day," Faith said. "I'm sure you have your hands full with your classes."

"No, that's fine," Laura replied, brushing a stray blonde hair away from her face. "It's been so long since I've been able to help in the library."

"Thanks for pitching in," Faith said.

"So what would you like me to do this morning?" Laura pointed to a cart of books. "Do you want me to reshelve them?"

"Fantastic. Thank you." Leaving Laura to her work, Faith returned to her desk.

She felt much better now. Except for the short notice, the tour assignment piqued her interest. What Nancy Drew enthusiast wouldn't be fascinated by the idea of hidden doors and passages?

Faith could start her research with the hand-drawn map in the display case and then dip back into the archives. She remembered seeing several references to the passages when she was preparing the display. Maybe the references were in one of the diaries. But she would have to be careful. Research had a way of captivating her, and she didn't have time to get lost in it.

She logged back on to her laptop and brought up her e-mail. Marlene hadn't sent the tour route, but she probably hadn't made it back to her office yet.

Faith opened a new document, loosened her shoulders, and shook out her hands. Then she checked the time. Piece of cake. It would even be enjoyable. She could do this—provided she didn't have too many interruptions.

The cat was always happy to demonstrate, for his human's benefit, ancient feline methods of dealing with stress and anxiety.

Now, for instance, he blocked all thoughts and studied his human. She was caught in one of her behavior loops—repeated finger tapping on the thing she called a keyboard—to the exclusion of admiring him. The cat had tried to show her that mastery of boxes and flat objects would only happen through more masterful movements—leaping into their midst, for example—but to no avail.

His person was muttering to herself, and he sensed she would benefit from another demonstration.

The cat prepared to launch himself onto her desk. Finally, he jumped, landing on top of the keyboard.

His human startled, then laughed. "You're an exceptional leaper, but you really are a complete and utter goofball."

The cat looked at her without moving.

"If you insist on helping, just keep the mouse pad warm and let me handle the keyboard. You're wise beyond your whiskers, but your spelling is atrocious."

As his person slipped back into her finger-tapping behavior loop, the cat decided it was time to resort to plan B—distraction through aerobic exercise. Calling upon his superior skills at improvisation, the cat set out to guide his human into a healthier activity.

Faith felt a commotion around her feet. Watson had found a catnip mouse and was giving it a workout. When he'd swatted it to where he couldn't reach it under the desk, he came and rubbed against her ankles with a plaintive mew.

She crumpled a piece of paper into a ball, tossed it to him, and went back to taking notes on a terrifying story she'd found about a footman who'd gotten lost in the manor's passageways.

Watson mewed from farther away, and she looked up. He stood in the doorway, rubbing his side against the doorframe.

Faith twiddled her fingers at him, then continued reading and taking notes.

He mewed again, and this time when she looked up, he capered out of the room.

She saved her work and went to the door, arriving in time to see his bobtailed rump disappear under a skirted table in the gallery. Clearly, he wanted to play a game of what Faith called "tailing."

"Would you like me to go after your cat?" Lois asked as she approached.

Faith tried to picture the tottery elderly woman, who had trouble finding her way from one room to another, trying to keep up with Watson in one of his playful moods. "No thank you, but it's kind of you to offer. Are you finding what you're looking for in our collections?"

Lois smiled. "I've found more treasure than I could possibly consume in a lifetime, but I wonder if you have any early Wilkie Collins."

Laura, passing with an armful of books, offered her assistance to Lois.

"Thank you," Lois said. "And Faith can go after her rascal, who I see peeking out from under that table skirt. He's an unusual cat."

"He's a very unusual cat," Faith agreed.

Lois peered at Watson. "If I didn't know better, I would say he wants to show you something."

Faith nodded. *Either Watson does indeed have something to show me or he has me completely wrapped around his little paw.* "Laura, I'll be right back."

Faith knew from long experience that in the game of tailing, she had to play by Watson's rules. They were simple enough: Watson ran ahead and hid, she followed, he jumped out to surprise her, and then he ran ahead again.

Faith tiptoed toward the skirted table, and just when she reached it and flipped the skirt up, Watson shot out the other end, dashed into the Main Hall, and careened around the corner into the music room.

Faith followed, hoping he hadn't just crashed his way into a colloquium program.

But all was quiet in the music room, and there was no evidence of a tuxedo cat—unless that twitching lump behind the drapes near the door to the salon had four white paws and two black ears.

This calls for furtive action. There was space behind the drapes due to the music room's unusual shape. Instead of opening the drape where Watson hid, she crept to the far end, slipped in behind, and sidled toward Watson, who had his back to her. "Tag, Watson, you're it."

Watson turned and lifted a paw to his mouth. He looked like he was shushing her.

Faith almost laughed. And then she became aware of voices in the salon. Unhappy voices coming nearer.

"It's my money, and I can do whatever I want with it," a woman snapped.

Faith wasn't sure she recognized the voice.

"That's not what I meant." A man.

Vic?

"If that's not what you meant, then why are you complaining?"

"I'm not complaining."

Vic and Nancy A. quarreling. This is awkward. Faith wanted to scoop up Watson and get out of there, but the voices were so close she was afraid she'd be seen, and that would be even more awkward. She shrank back as far as she could. She glanced at Watson. He'd tucked his paws. His ears and whiskers appeared alert.

"This is no more expensive than your trip to California last spring," Nancy A. reproached.

"That was a two-week trip," Vic spat back. "Two weeks, and I made solid contacts. This is six days of frittering and fantasizing—"

"Then why are you here?" Nancy A. demanded.

"Maybe I shouldn't be."

"Fine. See if I care."

"You will," Vic said.

Then Faith heard a door slam shut.

7

Faith listened intently. The air was stuffy and still behind the curtain in the music room but certainly not hot. Even so, a bead of sweat trickled down the back of her neck. She thought Vic had left the salon. *But did Nancy A. follow?*

She heard no more sounds, and then Watson blinked and came to twine around her ankles. For an all clear, it was good enough.

Faith shook her head at Watson and whispered, "That was *not* fun." Then she peeked carefully around the edge of the curtain and confirmed that they were alone, and the two of them returned to the library.

"I'm sorry for being gone so long," Faith told Laura.

"You weren't gone more than ten minutes," Laura said, giving her a strange look. "Is everything okay?"

"Everything's fine." *Except that it felt more like an eon, and I really did not want to hear that argument.* Faith pushed her thoughts away and changed the subject. "Were you able to find Wilkie Collins for Lois?"

"She's reading *The Moonstone*." Laura motioned toward the fireplace.

Lois had settled into one of the chairs there. As they watched, Watson hopped up into the chair next to her.

A couple of cronies, Faith thought with a smile.

"The other guest left, no one else arrived, and the books are reshelved."

"And I bet you'd like to take off into the beautiful morning."

Laura nodded. "But I'll come back after lunch."

"That sounds great. Thank you."

After Laura left, Faith sat at her desk and continued reading the footman's account of being lost in the manor's passageways. She felt a spider tickling the back of her neck as the poor man became more and more panicked.

She was glad to learn he'd returned unscathed to the downstairs kitchen. She also hoped he'd gone on to write fiction for a living, because she was fairly certain his hair-raising account was highly embellished if not entirely fabricated.

When Faith finished the story, she checked her e-mail. Marlene's message had arrived.

There's been a change of plans. To better accommodate our tours and not interfere with previously scheduled programs, we will now be giving the tours tomorrow at 1:00. This is good news, as it gives you more time to polish your script. I will inform Laura.

It was too bad she hadn't seen the e-mail before Laura left, but for Faith, it was even better news than Marlene realized. Faith wouldn't be able to give the tours after all. Tomorrow afternoon she had her own previously scheduled event—a webinar discussing archives in the digital age.

She replied to Marlene's e-mail, letting her know of the conflict. Then, to celebrate her reprieve, she saved the tour script and went back to designing her plan for cataloging the archives.

Faith's ex-beau in Boston had called her a control freak when she told him how much she liked organizing information. She'd tried to tell him it wasn't about control. It was about access—making it easier for people to find what they needed and sometimes information they hadn't even known they needed. That argument had marked the beginning of the end of their relationship. He'd found someone else he needed more than he needed her, and she'd found out that she didn't need him at all.

"Oh, the tragedy of misbegotten love and rescheduled tours, Watson."

Watson blinked one eye. Or was it a wink?

Later, when Faith's phone buzzed with a text from Midge inviting her to lunch at Snickerdoodles, she was once again surprised by how out of sync with time she could be.

"It just goes to show that time flies when you're having fun," she said to Watson. "Or in your case, time flies when you're having tunaroons."

Watson stared at her.

She laughed. "Don't worry. I'll pick some up for you while I'm in town."

Snickerdoodles Bakery & Tea Shop was next door to the Candle House Library in downtown Lighthouse Bay. The members of the Candle House Book Club often grabbed a treat or a hot drink at Snickerdoodles before their meetings at the library.

Today Faith met Midge Foster at the bakery. They beat the lunch rush and took their sandwiches, bowls of soup, and cups of tea to one of the tables facing the windows.

Midge was smart, compassionate, and funny and a comfortable person to be with. She was the concierge vet for the manor, and she also owned Happy Tails Gourmet Bakery located across the street from the Candle House Library. The bakery offered a wide variety of treats for pets, and tunaroons were Watson's favorite.

"So, how's your week going?" Midge asked. "I mean, besides a haunted staircase, the mystery of the disappearing man, and a mysterious letter."

Faith stopped with a spoon of mushroom soup halfway to her mouth.

"I saw Eileen at the library," Midge said with a chuckle. "It sounds like you're in for a lively time at the manor this week."

"I hope not."

Midge cocked her head. "That doesn't sound resoundingly positive."

"You get that look on your face when you're giving Watson a checkup," Faith said.

Midge grinned. "And Watson is just as good at wiggling away from me." Then she turned serious. "Is something going on?"

"More than usual when you get a large number of people together? I don't know, but I guess there's kind of a strange vibe with the group this week."

"Strange how?"

Faith took a bite of her sandwich. While she chewed it and chewed on Midge's question, the door opened and the two Nancies strolled inside the bakery. They both wore plaid skirts, sweaters, knee socks, and penny loafers.

The Nancies scanned the room. When they spotted Faith, they waved and walked over to her table.

"Hey! Small world," Nancy A. said. "Did you escape too?"

"Not that we aren't loving every catered minute at the manor," Nancy Z. chimed in.

"Castleton's a great place," Nancy A. agreed. "Full of great big egos. Why don't we grab some coffee and join you? You don't mind, do you?"

"Not at all," Midge said. When they'd gone to place their order, she whispered to Faith, "Would it matter if we did mind?"

"It's hard to say," Faith admitted. While they waited for the Nancies to join them, she filled Midge in on what she knew about them.

"So they're wild cards, but you like them," Midge summed up.

"Good diagnosis. I do like them. They're part of the strange vibe, but I like most of the people I've met this week."

Midge raised her brows. "Most?"

Faith nodded toward the Nancies coming back with muffins and cups of coffee.

"Did you talk about us while we were gone?" Nancy A. asked.

"Because we'd be disappointed if you didn't," Nancy Z. added.

"Then you'll be happy to know that Faith told me everything she knew and made up more besides." Midge raised her teacup to them. "I'm Midge Foster. When I'm not drinking tea, I'm the concierge vet at Castleton. If Togo needs anything while you're here, I'm just a phone call away."

"You even know the name of my dog," Nancy A. responded, then winked at Faith. "You *are* thorough."

"It sounds as though you two are enjoying yourselves at the colloquium," Midge said.

"We make a habit of enjoying ourselves everywhere," Nancy A. answered. "Also of enjoying ourselves at the expense of a few others. Bea for instance." She turned to Faith. "Did you tell her about Bea?"

"Bea Stapleton," Faith said to Midge. "She's the—"

"Oh, let me tell her." Nancy Z. rubbed her hands together with a wicked look in her eyes. "Bea Stapleton, retired professor of English who spent her formative, middle, and calcifying years at a small and not particularly influential college in Illinois. She invented the Nancy Drew Clue Colloquium single-handedly or with the help of her trusty sidekick, Paloma Martin, depending on which story you believe."

"Have you heard Bea pontificate about this sacred colloquium?" Nancy A. pulled her red glasses to the end of her nose, peering over them at Faith and Midge. "Bea says, and I happily misquote, 'We are a group comprised of significant scholars and only the finest fans, and we cherish the vastly valuable time we spend together poring over the oeuvre of Nancy Drew in perpetual pursuit of the most minuscule evidence proving the existence of social commentary in the classic canon.'" She drew several exaggerated breaths with a hand to her heart, then dropped her hand.

Nancy Z. clapped. "Well done."

"I hope you know I'm kidding." Nancy A. pushed her glasses back up her nose. "That is what Bea believes, but she's allergic to alliteration, and she'd get sick if she somehow stumbled and said it like that."

"Not to sound snooty or cynical, but why did you come to the manor for the colloquium?" Midge asked.

Nancy A. pointed at Midge. "You have the makings of a River Heights Roundtablian."

"They both do," Nancy Z. said. "Remember how Faith busted up our fight with the bee and the bird using only her smile and a plate of cookies? Guts and finesse—a killer combo."

"To answer your question," Nancy A. said to Midge, "we're here because we're the good-natured bad girls of Nancy Drew fandom. The Nancy Drew Clue Society might not like being called a fan club, but that's exactly what this whole thing is."

"And that's why we formed the River Heights Roundtable," Nancy Z. continued. "We embrace the evolution of Nancy Drew over the years. We revel in the thoroughly modern Nancy who emerged in the newer books. We love the excitement she exemplifies, and we're fond of the joy she represents."

"And you're dressed like her," Midge remarked. "Is everyone doing that or just you two?"

"Many people do," Nancy Z. said. "But not Bea. She's too long in the tooth to dress like the girl sleuth. Also, she's pretty well stuffed to the gills with scholarship, so she isn't able to bend and flow and be spontaneous like the rest of us. Even Paloma, the reigning Junior Miss Stuffy, gets into the cosplay."

"Bea's so-called scholarship is eternally fussy and self-important," Nancy A. said. "The real reason we're here is to help with that problem. We want to bring it all back down to earth. That's why we came up with the Roundtable too. It isn't a formal organization. No rule book for us. We're just chums who like to have fun."

"That's not a perfect rhyme, but this isn't a perfect world and you get the general idea." Nancy Z. glanced at her phone, then caught her cohort's attention. "We should get going."

"There's a big panel discussion this afternoon," Nancy A. explained. "It will offer opportunities aplenty for the well prepared. Nice to meet you, Midge. See you back at the ranch, Faith."

The two Nancies got up and hurried out the door.

Faith and Midge stared at each other.

"Opportunities for the well prepared?" Faith repeated.

"Back to that strange vibe you said is going on at the manor," Midge said. "I believe we might have found the epicenter."

"Now I can't make up my mind whether to pop into Bea's panel discussion for a few minutes or hide out in the cottage."

Midge shook her finger at Faith. "You can't fool me. You aren't wondering at all. You're going to that discussion because you can't wait to see what happens when the epicenter twins let loose."

Faith was grateful for Laura's availability and work ethic. She arrived after lunch, just as she'd said she would, even though the tours were postponed.

Faith left her studying for an exam and rushed to the music room, slipping in shortly before the colloquium's panel discussion started.

Lois, sitting in the back row, saw her and patted the empty chair next to hers. "Smart move, sitting back here," she said when Faith sat down. "It's closer to the refreshments."

Faith turned to see Brooke arranging plates on a table behind them. "I'm sure Brooke made something delicious again today."

"I was thinking more about how quickly you'll be able to grab a tray in case you need to intervene again." Lois pointed to the front. "The two Nancies are sitting right down there."

Faith stood up to see for herself. Bea and two other women sat at a draped table on a low stage, talking quietly. The two Nancies and Vic sat in the middle of the front row. Vic slouched a bit until Nancy A. nudged him with her shoulder.

Faith scanned the rest of the audience. She didn't see Bea's son, which didn't surprise her. Why would a guy in his early twenties be interested in a panel discussion about Nancy Drew? Except that he had come for the retreat, so maybe she was stereotyping.

As if to prove her bias, there was Ned Carson, a few years older than Drew, but still in his twenties. He'd taken a seat on the far end of a row toward the front of the room. Unlike so many in the audience, he looked at the panelists rather than a phone.

One of the tech guys on staff was in the side aisle, three rows back from the front, fiddling with a video camera on a tripod—no doubt checking the angle and focus to record the presentation. He'd set up another tripod and camera on the other end of that row to record from the opposite angle.

Faith knew that the manor offered video recordings of events, but if groups were interested in recordings they usually opted for the less expensive audio only. This setup for the colloquium was impressive.

Paloma went up on the stage and poured water for the presenters from a pitcher. She set the pitcher on the table and glided away. Then she appeared as though she couldn't quite decide where to sit—possibly because of the recording or the seats the Nancies had taken. She finally settled on the chair at the far end of the first row, first separating it a bit from the row.

As Faith sat back down, she wondered if Paloma was suffering from nerves or claustrophobia.

"Good afternoon," Bea said into a table microphone.

The murmurs and shufflings in the audience ceased.

"Thank you." Bea smiled. "Welcome to our panel discussion entitled 'Nancy Old and New.' Of course, it's no mystery that I am Bea Stapleton."

The audience laughed.

"Joining me this afternoon are Donna Webster from Warburton College and Andrea Greer from Pendleton Community College," Bea continued. "I will let Donna and Andrea further introduce themselves. But if I might just add"—she turned to Andrea—"it is especially nice to have someone from the Cape Cod education community taking part in our colloquium highlighting the region."

Applause started in Paloma's corner, and the audience joined in.

So far, so good, Faith thought. Maybe she'd worried over nothing. *Although what did I think was going to happen in the first five minutes?* She glanced at Lois.

The woman winked at her.

Has Watson been taking lessons from Lois?

"Thank you," Bea said. "If you have questions, please hold them until the end. Now, let's get started, shall we? We'll begin with you, Andrea. Tell us a bit about what the legacy of Nancy Drew means to you."

"For me, the legacy of Nancy is the gift of limitless mobility," Andrea said. "Hasn't she owned some fantastic cars? And if I heard right, some of you arrived in Nancy Drew cars. A blue roadster even." She glanced at Bea. "I know we're supposed to hold our questions until the end, but may I ask one now?"

"Question holding is for the audience. Special rules for panelists," Bea replied to general laughter.

"Does someone really have a blue roadster here?" Andrea asked, scanning the audience.

Nancy A. and Vic raised their hands. Then Nancy A. elbowed him, and he lowered his hand.

"I'm confused," Andrea said, studying the pair. "Which one of you brought the blue roadster?"

"I own it," Nancy A. announced. She motioned to Vic. "He came with me, and he wishes he owned it."

"I would kill for a ride in your car," Andrea said. "Can I have one?"

"Sure. Special rules for panelists—homicide not necessary," Nancy A. quipped. "I'll catch you when this is over."

"Don't tell him," Andrea said, pointing to Vic, "but you're my new BFF."

A few people in the crowd chuckled.

"Back to the legacy," Andrea continued. "Mobility isn't just about Nancy's cars. It's about her lifestyle too. She can go anywhere in the country. Anywhere in the world. She leads a red-carpet kind of life. A *magic* carpet life."

Bea nodded. "How did Nancy affect your life?"

"I grew up on Cape Cod in a working-class family. I was not part of the summerhouse and sailing set. Nancy held out her hand and said, 'Come with me.' In real life, magic carpets are few and far between, but even as a child, I knew that the ability to read is one of those magic carpets. So I read. I studied. I became the first in my family to graduate from college. And I went on to get my doctorate in English literature."

"That's wonderful," Bea said. "What did you do after college?"

"My degree offered me the mobility to teach anywhere," Andrea answered. "Big cities and parts unknown were very tempting. But I returned to my local community college so I could offer mobility to students coming up behind me."

The audience applauded.

"Were you the kind of girl who read under the covers with a flashlight?" Bea asked.

"I'd be disappointed to find out that any of us weren't," Andrea replied.

"Agreed. Thank you for inspiring us with your story," Bea said. "That was a touching tribute to our fictional heroine, to the women who have penned Nancy's stories over the years, and to the genius of Edward Stratemeyer."

"May I just add that I love the idea of limitless mobility?" Donna gestured around the room. "And look where that mobility has brought all of us today—to this colloquium in this incredible mansion."

"*And* a ride in a roadster," Andrea added, grinning. "I'm holding you to that, BFF."

"Hey, we can go now if you want," Nancy A. piped up. "Or we can talk about self-confidence, persistence, bravery, freedom, and independent spirit. All of those are character traits of our fictional heroine, and I'm willing to bet you have those traits too, because mobility alone didn't get you where you are today."

Now Faith wished she *had* moved closer to the front so she could see Bea's face better during Nancy A.'s interjections. From a distance, Bea appeared calm, and she'd undoubtedly learned how to deal with interruptions when she'd taught.

Faith rose slightly and glanced over at Paloma. She'd moved her chair a little more to the side and angled it so she probably had a good view of Bea and the Nancies. Was Paloma monitoring them or getting ready to referee?

Settling back into her seat, Faith felt her phone vibrate. She slipped it from her pocket and read a three-word text from Marlene.

The mystery letter.

8

"Is something amiss?" Lois whispered when she noticed Faith reading the text.

"I'm sure it's nothing," Faith assured her, not wanting to alarm—or overexcite—her elderly friend. "But I need to make a call."

"Should I save your seat?"

"No, that's all right. You can let someone else have it. I'll try to get back in time for the wrap-up."

Faith left the music room hoping Marlene's text really was nothing. The curiosity and slight anxiety behind that hope made her walk faster to reach the Main Hall. In that open space she could call Marlene without worrying about being overheard.

Wait a second. Why am I worried about being overheard? I'm obviously suffering from the Nancy Drew virus. She slowed down and punched in Marlene's number.

Marlene leaped into conversation before Faith even opened her mouth. "I've received some information. Where are you?" Marlene barked like a superintendent of detectives. Maybe the Drew virus was contagious and spreading.

"The Main Hall."

"My office, please."

"On my way." Faith didn't quite run from the hall, but she flew down the stairs to the basement and along the corridor to Marlene's office. She hurried in and stopped in front of Marlene's desk. "What is it?"

Marlene glanced up from her computer screen. "Sit down. No, wait. You'd better close the door."

Faith glanced up and down the hall before closing the door, and then she sat in one of the visitors' chairs in front of Marlene's desk.

Faith studied the assistant manager, wondering what this meeting was about. Marlene almost always looked serious, so her steady gaze didn't tell Faith anything. But Marlene seemed calm rather than ruffled, so Faith felt a layer of stress evaporate.

"I did as you suggested and put the letter in the safe last night," Marlene began.

When she didn't elaborate, Faith wondered if Marlene was waiting for her to comment, something she occasionally did. It was like a conversational game of cat and mouse—lay out tidbits of information but not quite enough, so the mouse had to scamper after them and keep asking questions.

"That's good," Faith finally replied. "Is there any news about the letter?"

Marlene frowned. "Someone claimed it this morning."

"But no one came forward last night at the dinner. So who was it?"

Marlene huffed. "I can't give out that kind of personal information."

"No, of course not. I'm glad it's been resolved, because I couldn't help worrying about it," Faith admitted. "But Bea and Drew and Paloma assumed it was a prop. Was it?"

Marlene stared down at her desk for a moment. "I honestly don't know. But if I did and if it wasn't a prop, then again, it wouldn't be my information to divulge."

Faith nodded.

"Why don't we leave it this way? As far as we're concerned, the letter is no longer a mystery," Marlene said. Then she eyed Faith. "Are you making progress on the script?"

A layer of stress settled back onto Faith's shoulders. "Yes, it's coming along. I'm enjoying the research."

"I thought you would."

"Did you get my e-mail about the conflict tomorrow afternoon?" Faith asked.

Marlene made a dismissive noise. "Aren't webinars usually offered on more than one date?"

"Often, yes, but tomorrow's the last date for this one. It's about archives in the digital age, and Wolfe insisted that I take it. He kindly offered to pay the $300 registration fee."

Marlene closed her eyes. "I'm beginning to wish I hadn't offered to do these tours, and frankly, I'm not willing to postpone them again. Working around the colloquium schedule is too difficult."

"I'm sorry that I won't be able to help," Faith said, "but I know the guests will enjoy them."

"They'll love them." Marlene sighed as she checked the clock. "I should pop into the panel discussion and see how it's going. But I'm sure it can't possibly be as exciting as our hidden passageways."

"I'll go with you," Faith offered. "I'd like to catch the last few minutes."

When they arrived at the music room, Faith realized the scene had changed dramatically since she had left. It appeared that Nancy A. had joined the panel. She stood on the low stage between Andrea and Donna, who were still seated. Neither of them seemed surprised or disturbed by Nancy A.'s presence. Bea was also standing on the stage, and she looked professional and resigned.

Faith scanned the room and noticed Paloma sitting in the back. She didn't see Vic anywhere.

"The Nancy Drew books are fiction," Nancy A. declared, "and Nancy Drew isn't real either. So take that piece of reality and stick it in your hollow oak and smoke it." She sat down, then jumped up again. "Wait. I'm not finished. Stand up, Z. Stand up and stand proud."

Nancy Z. stood and faced the audience, raising her chin and planting her fists on her hips in a triumphant superhero pose. "I can't add anything to your very cogent comments."

"I was wrong," Marlene whispered to Faith. "I hope the tours aren't this exciting. With those two on the loose, we might have to break up a fistfight."

"Then why don't you sit down?" Bea asked.

"I have no *comments*," Nancy Z. continued, "but I do have a question.

In all your lengthy discussion of the classic canon and discrepancies and whatnot, why didn't you mention one of the most fascinating puzzles of all—the elusive location of River Heights?"

"That might have gotten lost in the shuffle," Andrea responded.

"My friend Nancy A. does have a reputation for creating shuffle," Nancy Z. said. "But there's another explanation. It's more nefarious, and it's all about squashing rivals."

"Oh, for the love of—" Bea sat down and started gathering her papers. Her face was blank, as though the program had ended and everyone had left the room but her.

"They didn't want to bring up Nancy's hometown," Nancy Z. went on, "because if they did, it would remind all of you about us—the River Heights Roundtable. We're the fun-loving Nancy nuts, the dynamic Drew divas, the ones who deal in truth about the premier girl sleuth. For some reason I cannot fathom, they feel threatened by us. Their self-image, their whole raison d'être, becomes shuffled by our appearance."

Bea checked the table and floor as though searching for stray belongings. She picked up her papers and put her purse on her shoulder, ignored startled looks from Donna, Andrea, and everyone else, and walked out of the room.

Faith turned to locate Paloma and jumped. Paloma was standing directly behind her.

"They aren't a fan club. They're a gang." With that, Paloma marched out too.

Lois joined Faith and Marlene as the other guests descended on the brownies and cupcakes Brooke had artfully arranged on the refreshment table.

"I don't know whether I was more surprised or disappointed at that very abrupt ending to their lively discussion," Lois said.

Faith guessed Lois was disappointed. She hadn't had an opportunity yet to find out Lois's background, but she decided to make that happen before the colloquium ended. *And I hope she tells me she's a retired spy. Or she always wanted to be one.*

A hoot of laughter came from a small group gathered around Andrea, Donna, and the two Nancies.

Marlene glanced at them and shook her head.

"Would you like me to get you a brownie or a cupcake?" Faith asked Lois. "Or a brownie *and* a cupcake?"

"You know me so well already," Lois said, her eyes twinkling. "I'll go thank the panelists." She headed over to the small group.

Faith approached the refreshment table and smiled when she read the names of the desserts: Bungalow Brownies and Velvet Mask Cupcakes. Then she sidled up to Brooke. "Everything looks scrumptious, and I love the names."

Brooke grinned. "Thanks. They're my own concoctions. I didn't use the cookbook this time. So how did the panel discussion go?"

"From what I witnessed, it was quite interesting," Faith answered as she fixed a plate for Lois.

Before Brooke could respond, Marlene appeared and scrutinized the refreshment table. She turned to the sous-chef. "Are there any more cupcakes?"

"Yes, in the kitchen. I'll get them." Brooke hurried away.

Lois was still talking to the panelists, so Faith joined the group and handed Lois the plate.

"Thank you. No treats for you?" Lois asked.

"I don't dare try everything Brooke makes," Faith said, "even though I would love to."

"I hear you," Nancy A. said. "I know just the treat for you. Why don't you have what these two are having?" She motioned to Andrea and Donna. "I'm taking them for rides in my roadster. Would you care for a spin in my baby too?"

"That would be great," Faith replied.

They made plans to meet at the guest garage after Faith locked up the library for the day.

After telling Lois she hoped to see her later, Faith returned to the library.

Laura, engrossed in a textbook that might have broken her toe if she dropped it, glanced up, lifted a hand in a brief wave, and immediately bent her head to her reading again.

Faith smiled. *A student destined to go far.*

She scanned the library and noticed Bea and Paloma sitting in front of the fireplace. Watson sat in a chair next to them. All three appeared calm and content.

Faith walked over and sat down.

"Afternoon tea is a civilized ritual," Bea said, raising her hand to her mouth as though she had a teacup. "But in truth, a library is the best kind of refreshment."

"There are times when I think of the library as my place of refuge," Faith said. "I'm glad to find you both here. I see you've met my cat. Watson, it was kind of you to share your chairs."

"He's the perfect host, and if he's like my Snowball, he's also your BFF." Bea laughed and shook her head. "I shouldn't have walked out of the panel. It was poor form."

"*They* have no form," Paloma said.

"Are you worried they'll continue to cause problems?" Faith asked.

"They won't if we don't let them," Paloma answered.

Bea put a hand on Paloma's arm. "What she means is, they won't because we'll try—or try harder—to not let them know when they get to us."

"Or how annoying and petty they are. But I will try." Paloma closed her eyes and took several deep breaths. When she opened her eyes, she said, "Faith, I want to tell you how much we appreciate the Drew extras the staff planned for us. The mysterious letter at dinner last night and then the tapping heels in the hallway outside my room later on."

"Tapping heels?" Faith repeated. "You mean, like—"

"Straight out of *The Clue of the Tapping Heels*."

Faith turned to Bea. "Did you hear them?"

"Sadly, no."

"Maybe you'll hear them tonight," Paloma said.

"So what happened?" Faith asked.

"The tapping heels woke me, and at first I thought I might be dreaming. But then I got into it, and I wrote the pattern down in case it's part of a bigger puzzle." Paloma studied Faith's face for a second. "But I can see you aren't going to give anything away. I showed the pattern to Drew, and he told me it said, 'SOS,' 'Beware,' and 'LOL.'"

"And I told Paloma that Drew doesn't know Morse code," Bea said.

"Even so," Paloma went on, "the tapping is inventive and fun, so thank you."

"I'll be sure to pass that along," Faith said, hoping she didn't sound or look as mystified as she felt. She was fairly certain the Drew extras hadn't been planned by Castleton staff.

There was a human in the manor who walked on silent cat feet.

At first the cat had welcomed this person as a fellow traveler. The cat appreciated the fact that this human avoided louder humans and did not keep company with a dog. But then this most feline of humans disappointed the cat by making his way to the ocean's edge, removing portions of his clothing, and letting his feet get wet.

Such antithetical behavior put the cat on high alert. Here was a person who needed watching.

But only after careful napping.

When Faith stopped by the guest garage for her roadster ride, she found Vic there instead of Nancy A. She didn't have to say hello, ask where Nancy was, or make small talk. Vic took care of everything.

"Hey, good to see you," Vic said. "Nancy will be down in a few. She asked me to show you a good time till she gets here. Did she tell you how we met? It was like an old movie. We were at an auction, bidding against each other for this baby." He patted the roadster's fender. "And I tell you, when I saw this fabulous piece of machinery, it was love at first sight. It looks authentic, don't you think? But it drives like the modern wonder it is. It even has a keyless ignition."

Faith was wondering if she would rather skip the ride to escape the onslaught of information when Nancy A. arrived.

"Vic, honey," Nancy A. said, and he immediately stopped talking. "Run back and get my letter sweater, will you? I forgot it."

"Sure, babe."

"Thanks, lamb." As soon as he was gone, Nancy A. tossed her key fob into the air and caught it in the palm of her hand. It was embossed with the classic Nancy Drew silhouette. "For luck." She tucked the fob into her pocket, and then she pointed at the car. "Hop in."

As soon as they climbed into the roadster, Nancy A. revved the engine. Then she sped off, her laughter trailing behind them.

"I agree with Andrea about books being magic carpets," Nancy A. said, turning onto a wooded lane, "but this car is my piece of enchanted rug. It's better than a book, because it takes me places in real time in real life. It lets me escape."

Later that evening Faith enjoyed her own kind of escape by taking a stroll around the grounds with Watson. Some evenings they wandered, but tonight he seemed to know exactly where he wanted to go. He headed for the guest garage, and Faith was about to apologize for taking a ride in the roadster without him when she heard something.

Watson stopped, but Faith continued forward.

Ned stood rigidly against the wall next to Nancy A.'s open garage door. He stared into the distance, making an eerie, high-pitched moan.

"Ned?" Faith said.

He startled and looked around as though disoriented. When he noticed her standing there, he didn't say a word. He simply pointed into the garage bay.

Faith stumbled into the garage, forcing herself to approach the still figure in the driver's seat and feel for a pulse.

She couldn't find one.

Nancy A. was dead.

9

Faith rushed out of the garage. She wanted to reverse time and hop into the roadster next to Nancy A., hear her rev the engine and laugh as she headed for the open road to escape.

Watson nudged her ankle with his head, and she bent to pick him up.

Nancy A. would never again hold Togo in her arms or hear him yip. Never scratch behind his ears, never shush Vic. She would never again escape. After burying her face in Watson's soft fur, Faith knew she had to pull herself together and see this nightmare through.

Struggling to hold Watson with one arm, Faith shakily fished her phone out of her pocket with her free hand and dialed 911. The operator asked her a string of questions, and she answered them the best she could.

Watson started squirming in her arms, so she set him down.

Then she called Marlene and Wolfe. The call to Wolfe went straight to voice mail. Marlene said she would come right away.

As she waited, Faith wrapped her arms around herself and gazed into the dark night sky, past the moon and the stars.

Marlene arrived before the ambulance from Lighthouse Bay. "You're sure it's Nancy Allerton? And you're sure she's gone?" she asked, not venturing close enough to see for herself.

Faith nodded. She didn't blame Marlene for not entering the garage.

"Thank you for calling me," Marlene said.

"Of course." Faith cleared her throat. "I called Wolfe too, but he didn't answer. Do you know where he is?"

"I assume that's his business and not ours." Marlene motioned to Ned. "What did he have to say?"

Ned must have heard her because he staggered over, still looking shaky.

"What were you doing out here?" Marlene asked him.

"I was taking a walk to the beach," Ned explained. "When I went past the garage, I heard a car running."

"And you stopped to check on it. That was the right thing to do," Faith said.

"Well, no." Ned stared at the ground. "I didn't."

"You didn't see if Nancy A. was all right?" Marlene sounded aghast. "Why on earth not?"

"Because I wasn't paying attention," Ned answered. "I didn't know the car was in the garage. In Boston, I hear cars everywhere all the time, and I don't think twice about them."

"So when did you make the discovery?" Marlene pressed.

"It was when I came back from the beach and the car was still running that it clicked. It didn't seem right, because, you know, closed door, running car, carbon monoxide—" Ned stopped, looking as though he was reliving that horrible realization.

"What did you do?" Marlene asked.

Her question seemed to jolt Ned out of his thoughts, and he shook himself. "I wasn't sure what to do, so I checked the door. It wasn't locked and I opened it. Nancy was slumped over the steering wheel. I ran in and shut off the engine. I guess I got light-headed from the fumes, but I made it outside, and then you must have come along." He glanced at Faith.

"How are you feeling now?" Faith asked.

"I'll be okay." Ned rubbed his forehead with his fingertips. "Do you think I could have saved her if I had stopped the first time?" His face was ashen, and it appeared that he might be sick. "Oh, man."

"I can't believe you didn't," Marlene said.

"It didn't occur to me," Ned snapped. "I guess it shows I wouldn't make a good sleuth. I'm generally not a suspicious person." He walked away from them.

Away from Marlene, anyway, Faith thought.

"There's more than suspicion involved in something like this," Marlene muttered. "He needs to work on common sense too."

Faith heard sirens in the distance. Then an ambulance followed by a police cruiser raced down the same long drive that she and Nancy A. had sped along that afternoon.

Escaping on her magic carpet.

By the time the EMTs and Officers Bryan Laddy and Mick Tobin climbed out of their vehicles, curious guests were arriving on the scene too.

At first, the officers established a boundary to keep people from coming any closer to the garage bay. As more guests appeared, they finally asked everyone to return to the manor, enlisting Faith and Marlene to help them shepherd the group back inside.

But the police hadn't been able to keep the guests from seeing where the EMTs had parked the ambulance and which garage bay was garishly lit by the rotating lights. Word spread, and when Vic and Nancy Z. finally raced out of the manor, they obviously knew whose car occupied that bay.

Nancy Z. grabbed Vic's shoulder. "You came down without her. She's upstairs, right? Where is she?"

"Ma'am, we need you to go back inside," Officer Laddy said, adjusting his glasses.

"Is that where she is?" Nancy Z. turned around, looking wildly up at the manor, at the windows, and at the faces peering out.

Making a sound like a low growl, Vic tried to muscle past Tobin. But the officer, who used to be a wrestler in college, had no trouble stopping him, and Vic's growl turned into an anguished howl.

Then an unexpected angel swooped in. Bea brushed past Marlene and went to Nancy Z. She put her arms around the distraught woman and held her as she sobbed. "I'll take her up to her suite and stay with her."

"Thank you," Faith said, touched by Bea's compassionate reaction to the crisis. She watched Bea gently lead Nancy Z. away.

Officer Laddy approached Faith and Marlene. "We'll need to

take a look at Ms. Allerton's room." He nodded toward Vic. "Is he the husband?"

Vic stood quietly now and appeared shrunken next to Tobin.

"Fiancé," Marlene offered.

Ned went to Vic and reached out to touch his arm. "Hey, man—"

Vic pulled away. "Nancy was just going for a drive. It's what she liked to do. She liked walking the dog too. I'll get Togo and take him out. Does anyone have any objections?"

Officer Tobin put his hand on Vic's shoulder.

Vic flinched but walked next to Tobin to the manor.

"I can't believe it." Faith felt as though she'd been saying it nonstop all night, although she knew she'd only been saying it over and over in her head for—she glanced at the clock—not even two hours? But she had to say it out loud again. "I can't believe it. Nancy A. didn't seem like the kind of person who would do something like this."

After all the guests had been ushered away from the garage and back to the manor, Officers Tobin and Laddy had followed Faith and Marlene to the library. Faith had texted Brooke, and her friend had quickly joined them, bearing a pot of fresh coffee and leftover brownies.

"We don't know that she did it," Officer Laddy said. He blew a breath into his hands and rubbed them, though he'd just had them around a cup of coffee and they couldn't be cold. "I've read about death by carbon monoxide poisoning, but reading about it doesn't prepare you for seeing it in real life."

Faith knew Bryan Laddy went by the book and wouldn't make a statement about a case that he couldn't back up with facts. He was the youngest member of the Lighthouse Bay Police Department, and this wasn't the first time she'd seen him get a little rattled.

"Could it have been an accident?" Faith asked.

"Maybe," Tobin said. "It makes you wonder, doesn't it? Didn't she know better than to sit in a running car in a closed garage? But we can't say anything for sure until we get the results of the autopsy."

"Vic and Nancy Z. are both so broken up," Faith remarked. "I hope they'll be all right."

"It's a tough thing to deal with," Officer Tobin said. "Her fiancé had the right instinct to take the dog for a walk."

"Doing the ordinary helps you through times that are extraordinary," Brooke said. "I read that somewhere. It's a way to cope. Walking the dog. Making coffee."

"Vic has been gone a long time." Marlene turned to the officers. "Do we have to worry if he doesn't come back soon?"

"I don't think you need to worry about anything else tonight," Tobin replied, getting to his feet. "But if he isn't here in the morning, go ahead and give us a call."

The cat rejoined his human as she unlocked the front door, circling her ankles in the ritual practiced by cats since the beginning of human domesticity.

He did not always hold with the ancient ways, as many of them spoke more of hunting and survival than of snug rooms and napping. But the ankle ritual made sense even in this modern era of cans that opened without can openers. By circling his human's ankles, he undid the travails and burdens of her day.

He accompanied her inside, making sure to continue his circling so that she picked her feet up in the pantomime of shedding troubles that might trip her as she went.

When they arrived safely in the living room, the cat presented his chin so she could show her thanks.

Faith rubbed Watson's chin. "Thank you as always for the circle dance on the way in. Someday we might both end up on our faces, but it hasn't happened yet, and with luck and agility it never will."

The cat purred.

"My goodness, what a wretched evening." She dropped into her comfy chair, feeling so drained she couldn't muster the energy to think about getting ready for bed. "And there are still dishes in the sink from supper," she told the ceiling.

Watson meowed.

Faith switched her gaze to Watson, who was looking handsome and hopeful on the hearth rug. "I did say supper, didn't I? And there's a bag of tunaroons with your name on it in the cupboard."

Watson trotted to the kitchen.

She pried herself out of the chair and followed him. "You know what else we have in here? Ice cream." She placed a tunaroon into Watson's bowl and put a scoop of salted caramel mocha ice cream into a bowl for herself.

They ate their treats companionably, and then she took care of the dishes while Watson took care of his paws and ears.

When kitchen and cat were tidy, they returned to the living room.

Faith picked up a notebook and pen before sitting down again. "You've seen me in this state before, haven't you? But this is going to be better than trying to sleep right now. You're welcome to curl up in my lap if you want to."

After Watson was settled in her lap, she opened the notebook and jotted down everything she could remember about the evening. First she wrote the basic facts in one long paragraph and then she added the details, including conversations, impressions, and questions.

When Faith couldn't think of anything else to write, she closed the notebook. The writing was enough for now, and by closing the cover, maybe she would be able to close her eyes and sleep.

The next morning Faith headed to the dining room to check on Vic and Nancy Z. Nancy A.'s death had been a shock, and she wondered how they were coping with the tragedy and if she could do anything to help.

She found Marlene standing in the corridor outside the door of the dining room. She was glad to see that they had the same instinct.

"I feel slightly ghoulish peeking in at the guests like this," Marlene admitted.

"Are you going to say anything to them?" Faith asked.

"You mean address them as a group?" Marlene backed away from the door. "Oh no. I think that's for Bea Stapleton or someone from the colloquium to do."

Faith realized they might not be here out of the same instinct.

"I sent an e-mail to each of the guests before I went home last night," Marlene continued. "Just the facts to keep rumors in check. And I certainly don't think they need me to stop at each table and offer my condolences. That couldn't help but sound hollow. I'd hardly met the woman."

"I thought you might be here to give an announcement," Faith said.

"No, I came to make sure Vic got back last night."

"It was kind of you to check on him," Faith replied.

Marlene sniffed. "I didn't want to have to call the police again."

Faith sighed. They definitely weren't here out of the same instinct.

"Do you know what surprised me last night?" Marlene asked. "Or who surprised me?"

Faith shook her head.

"Didn't you notice who wasn't there through all the chaos and afterward?" Marlene frowned. "And here I thought you were such a natural-born sleuth. Now you've surprised me too. It's Paloma."

How did I miss that last night? I even wrote everything down when I got home. Faith glanced into the dining room and spotted Paloma sitting at a table with Bea and several others.

"She was conspicuously absent for all of it. Not that it means anything. It's not as if they liked each other." Marlene turned and headed down the hallway.

Faith watched Marlene walk away, hesitating now over her own reason for coming to the dining room. *Am I being ghoulish?*

Then she saw Lois waving her in. When Faith entered, the aromas of French toast, bacon, and coffee created an illusion of coziness, even coming from so large and ornate a room. The clatter of cutlery, murmur of voices, and occasional soft laugh were the sounds of life continuing to go on.

As she made her way through the room, guests greeted her and smiled and put out hands to pat her as though she might need comfort too. She stopped to thank Bea for her kindness to Nancy Z. Then she stopped to give Nancy Z. a hug.

Vic sat alone at a nearby table. He was hunched over a cup of coffee. When another guest put a hand on his shoulder in passing, he recoiled.

Faith was going to approach Vic, but after witnessing his reaction, she changed her mind. Instead, she poured a cup of coffee from the buffet and sat down next to Lois.

They watched Vic shrug off another approach from a guest.

"Sharing comfort in times of tragedy—it's the natural way of things, don't you think?" Lois said. "But giving is so often easier than receiving."

"That poor guy."

Lois nodded. "Do we know what happened yet?"

"I haven't heard anything official."

"Carbon monoxide is what people are saying."

"That's probably close enough for now."

"The rest of the talk has been equal parts shock, sadness, and the hope that the colloquium will continue without interruption."

"How did you find all that out?" Faith asked.

"I've been to the buffet several times and visited with friends at other tables," Lois admitted. "It doesn't do to sit too long at my age."

"And there's nothing wrong with your hearing."

"Nothing whatsoever." Lois pointed behind Faith. "Bea told us she'd have something to say."

Bea stood, and the room grew quiet.

Faith noticed that Vic still sat over his coffee cup, but he'd turned slightly toward Bea.

"My friends," Bea said, "sadly, we've lost one of our own through a tragic accident. But someone pointed out to me this morning that it was appropriate she died with her Nancy Drew on. Nancy A., you were a true original, and you will be missed." She paused for a moment. "Now someone else asked if our programs will continue as scheduled. The answer is an absolute yes. Are there any other questions?"

A hand went up, and a voice called out, "I've heard that it isn't possible for a modern car engine to put out enough carbon monoxide to kill someone."

"Roadsters are vintage," someone answered.

"No, not this one," Bea replied. "The car isn't a genuine antique. It's been so heavily restored it might as well be brand-new. She only let you believe it was real."

With a sharp intake of breath, Nancy Z. was on her feet. "That was incredibly insensitive."

"You're right," Vic spoke up. "It isn't real. Just like none of the rest of your Nancy Drew fantasy is real. The only thing real is your condescension toward *my* Nancy. There, I bet you didn't think I knew a long word like that. Here's something else I know. Can the exhaust from a modern engine kill you? The answer is an absolute yes."

The cat knew he had superior sensitivity. Truly, he was almost too sensitive for his own good. Recognizing this was not a character flaw, nor was it a source of pride. It merely was.

The large manor where he spent many precious hours must have been constructed with a sensitive cat in mind. There were numerous nooks and crannies to explore. The dark pathways between rooms and floors gave the cat private passage without setting paw on cold marble, allowing him to escape dogs and other annoying visitors with ease.

But already this morning his first nap had been disturbed by one of the dogs. The cat, even though wakened by a cold nose to his posterior, swatted the nose only once. He'd then offered his condolences, this being the canine who had lost his human the night before.

Of course, the dog only focused on his swatted nose and ran yipping around the room. The noise made further attempts at napping impossible.

The cat's second nap, in the sun-filled lounge on the second floor, was interrupted by the human named for an insect and the one she called her son. They exchanged stinging words about accomplishments and regrets and, most ironically, about compassion, which they did not show toward a cat and his nap.

He had to slink away. He disappeared from the lounge and reappeared in the room where humans played with paper and fabric and lovely pieces of yarn. Now the room was blessedly empty and quiet, and there were plenty of boxes and baskets for a sensitive cat to sleep in.

Unfortunately, the third nap was not the charm. The cat was rudely brought out of slumber yet again but not by a yelp or a yell. This time he wakened to an extremely small sound and a tantalizing smell. The sound skittered to his sensitive ears, making them swivel. The smell left a trail for his sensitive nose to follow.

Ears and nose led him to a cupboard in a corner of the room. He tried to pull the cupboard door open with his paw. And tried again. And again.

Then he gave up and went to find his human with her useful opposable thumbs.

10

Faith listened to the howling wind trying to get through the French doors in the library. The wind had ushered in gray skies and damp, but try as they might, none of the three could get into her snug sanctuary. Faith pulled her sweater tighter around her anyway, as much to keep out the somber mood that had descended on the manor as to keep out the cold.

While she finished writing the script for Marlene's passageway tours, she received calls from Midge and Aunt Eileen, both of them shocked and sympathetic over Nancy A.'s death.

"Is someone looking after her dog?" Midge asked.

"Vic, her fiancé."

"Is he okay with that?"

"As far as I know."

"I'll check with Marlene. He might not even be sticking around the rest of the week, but if he is, I'd like him to know we're here for him and the dog."

Eileen sounded more concerned about Faith. "Did you find her?"

"No, thank goodness."

"But you felt for her pulse—"

"Where did you hear that?" Faith interrupted.

"It isn't true?"

"It is, but where did you hear it?"

"This morning at Snickerdoodles. News travels fast around here. You know that."

"I'm just wondering who from Castleton has already been in town talking about it."

"Does it matter?" Eileen asked.

"I'm not sure," Faith admitted.

"I heard it was either an accident or suicide," Eileen went on. "Is there some question?"

"I find it hard to believe that Nancy A. would commit suicide. She was bubbling over with life. Yesterday afternoon she gave me a ride in her roadster, and she talked about luck and magic. And escaping."

"We don't always see the signs," Eileen said.

Faith sighed. "I know."

"Please take care of yourself."

When she disconnected from the call, Faith saw Watson sitting in front of her, waiting his turn for her attention. "You're so handsome in your patience, even if you are impolite enough to listen in on private conversations. What can I do for you?"

Watson stretched and yawned.

"Nap time already?"

Suddenly he leaped into the air, scampered to the display case, and peered at her from behind one of the legs as though it hid him perfectly.

She laughed. "You trickster."

Watson ran for the door and glanced back at her.

No guests were in the library, so Faith gave in, locked the door, and another game of tailing was on. This morning's chase became a marathon effort, taking them through the Great Hall Gallery, into the Main Hall, down a corridor to the banquet hall, out of the banquet hall and into the billiard room, and finally into the crafts room.

Watson stopped and sat in the corner, lifting his chin to her.

"Cornered at last," Faith said and sat on the floor beside him. "Poor Togo, though. Life isn't always fair. It isn't fair, and it doesn't always give us what we want. Sometimes we have to hunt and chase after happiness until we find it, don't we?"

Watson rubbed the side of his face against her knee, then turned and rubbed it against the cupboard door and meowed.

"Silly boy, do you think there's something in there for the winner of the first annual tailing marathon?"

Watson meowed again.

She opened the cupboard, wondering what he would do when faced with plastic bins of craft supplies.

Naturally he found a cat-size space on the second shelf up and immediately fit himself into it. He all but disappeared into the darkest corner.

"Rumpy, you should probably come out."

He didn't.

"Are you ignoring me? What are you doing back there?" Faith heard a small scraping noise. "Oh, I see what you're up to."

Watson's face appeared and then his paw. He pushed a coin from the edge of the shelf onto the floor.

"What is it with cats and the need to knock things off shelves?"

Watson's paw went back to work, and two more coins joined the first one on the floor. And then a key fob.

Faith gasped. The key fob bore the silhouette of Nancy Drew, and it looked just like the one Nancy A. had used for her roadster.

She called the police station in Lighthouse Bay. While she waited to be connected to an officer, she marveled at the interesting turn her life had taken when she came to live at Castleton. She wondered how many librarians could say they knew all the police officers in town. It wasn't an accomplishment she'd ever expected to claim.

Officer Jan Rooney took the call. In her early forties, she was a smart, solid officer. "Miss Newberry, how may I help you?"

"I have a question about last night. You know about what happened—"

"Yes, I am aware of the incident at the manor."

"Did Officer Tobin or Officer Laddy find a key fob in the car last night? Or in Nancy A.'s pocket?"

"You're referring to the victim?"

"Sorry, yes. Nancy Allerton, Nancy A. We also have a Nancy Z. for Ziegler staying here."

"Thank you for clarifying. But you're asking about a key fob for a 1930s roadster?"

"The car's been extensively rebuilt, and there's some debate over whether it can really be called a 1930s car anymore, although it looks like one—"

Officer Rooney cleared her throat.

Faith admonished herself for rambling. *I was beginning to sound just like Vic.* "It has a keyless ignition."

"I haven't seen the full report yet," Officer Rooney said. "Let me go get it. Just a moment."

While Faith waited for the officer to return, she scooped up the fob and coins with a piece of card stock she found on a table. She wondered if the local forensic technicians could lift paw prints from solid objects and what they would look like.

Watson had lost interest in the cupboard and was now sitting in the window, watching the wind playing a game of tailing with the leaves.

"Miss Newberry? No key fob is listed in the report. No car keys either."

"Really? Then how did they think the car could be running when Ned found it? Unless they thought he took the key fob?"

"Those are good questions," Officer Rooney said. "As I wasn't a responding officer on the case, I'll have to get back to you on them. It could be it was inadvertently omitted from the report. Now I have a question for you. Why are you asking about a key fob?"

"Watson discovered a key fob with a silhouette of Nancy Drew on it that looks like the one Nancy A. had," Faith explained. "It was in a cupboard in the crafts room."

"The Nancy Drew silhouette is something of an icon, isn't it? The fob might be a sample for the craft session associated with this colloquium. Do you think that's possible?"

"Brooke did put edible Nancy Drew silhouettes on cookies Sunday afternoon."

"I appreciate your call and your concern, and I don't want you to think I'm dismissing this. Hold on to the fob. I'll speak to Officers Tobin and Laddy, and someone will get back to you."

"I haven't touched the fob, but Watson's paw prints are on it. I'll put it in a plastic bag."

"That's fine. Thank you. Again, someone will be in touch." Officer Rooney hung up.

"She thought I was joking about your prints," Faith said to Watson as she searched for a plastic bag. She found one meant for jewelry hardware and slipped the fob into it. "And that's just as well, because I don't want them pulling you in for paw prints and questioning."

Faith was glad Officer Rooney took her seriously. She knew that some of her ideas might qualify as flights of fancy more than they did as theories.

This one, for instance—what if the police hadn't found a key fob because the car hadn't been running just before she and Watson happened on the scene? She believed Ned when he told her he'd turned the car off.

But what if he was lying?

Marlene clapped. "All right, everyone, gather around."

Faith listened to the delighted guests as Marlene revealed the hidden door near the fireplace. She almost regretted not leading the tours. Almost. But the webinar topic was interesting, timely, and a great opportunity for professional development.

She watched them go, then readied her laptop for the short trip to the cottage. If she tried to concentrate on the webinar here, interruptions were guaranteed.

"Watson, are you coming with me?"

The cat stayed put where he sat handsomely on the display case.

"Declining my invitation? Then I'm leaving you as the librarian in charge, although I'm sorry to say that I won't be trusting you with the keys." She locked the door behind her. Marlene would let her tour groups in and out of the library with her own keys.

When Faith returned to the library after the webinar, Watson was either still or once again sitting handsomely atop the display case.

"Job well done, sir. Remind me to put in for a raise for you." Faith rubbed the cat between the ears. "Did you practice good customer service and move aside if Marlene's tourists wanted to see what you're sitting above like the great tuxedoed lump?"

Watson blinked at her and jumped down, revealing a small, rectangular empty space in the display case.

Faith studied the case for a moment. Then she realized the hand-drawn passageway map was missing. Wolfe's father had drawn the map when he was a child, and its only real value was sentimental. But she would feel terrible if she didn't find it. The last thing she wanted to do was let Wolfe and the rest of the Jaxon family down.

Faith rarely panicked or grew hysterical, and she knew that she couldn't let the missing map drive her in that direction. She hadn't panicked the night before in a more dire situation. She stopped, breathed, and focused.

Then she texted Brooke. *Any Bungalow Brownies left? Breakdown avoidance necessary.*

A reply came within seconds. *On it.*

While Faith waited for her friend, she examined the case more closely. Nothing else appeared to be missing. She thought about the last time she'd seen the map. It was yesterday morning when Wolfe was inspecting the display.

A few minutes later, Brooke breezed in, handed Faith a plate covered with a paper napkin, and headed for the door again.

"Wait," Faith said.

"No time or the perfection in the oven will no longer be perfect."

"Thanks. You're an angel."

"Then please spread the word to every handsome devil you meet." Brooke grinned and left.

"Did you hear that, Watson? You're the handsomest devil I know." Faith locked the library door, stepped through the French doors to the tiled loggia, and quickly indulged her "panic tooth." While she absorbed the chocolate and sugar with a hint of espresso, she thought the situation through, turning possibilities over in her mind.

Now that she was thinking more calmly, she realized the most likely possibility involved Marlene, who was due to be finishing the last tour—she checked the time on her phone—in ten or fifteen minutes.

The last tourists arrived back in the library, thanking Marlene and telling her they were ready for another passageway adventure anytime.

Faith was glad the tours were such a hit. Maybe Marlene's good mood would last through her questions about the map.

"What map?" Marlene asked when Faith tried to tell her about it. Marlene was apparently basking in her tour guide glory and possibly not taking in details the way she usually did. "How is it my problem if you've misplaced a map?"

She was beginning to regret suspecting Marlene. "I didn't say it was. I'm just letting you know that a map is missing from the display case.

The hand-drawn map of the passageways. Actually, I was wondering if you borrowed it for the tours."

Marlene shot a glance toward the display case. Watson was sitting on it again. "Is the cat able to get into the case?"

"No."

"Then I'm afraid I can't help you. But you can let me know when you find it again." Marlene crossed her arms. "Are you sure you locked the case?"

"Yes."

"Is anything else missing?"

Faith shook her head.

"Maybe you didn't lock the case," Marlene argued. "Why did you have the map on display in the first place? I'm sure Wolfe won't be pleased. He might not be so quick to recommend webinars in the future. I suggest that you take the time to discover the facts before accosting innocent people. I'm sure I'm not the only one who doesn't appreciate being accused." She turned and stormed out of the library.

Faith scooped up Watson from the display case and cuddled him. He rubbed his head along her jaw.

"We have a mystery on our paws, Watson. Another one is more like it." She put him back on the display case. "Look around, will you, and tell me if you find anything that smells like a clue."

"It sounded to me like *she* was the one doing the accusing."

Faith spun around, startling Nancy Z. as much as Nancy Z. had startled her. "I'm so sorry," Faith said. "I hadn't realized anyone was here."

"I was on the tour because Nancy A. was looking forward to it. But then . . ." Nancy Z. wiped her cheek with the back of her hand, and Faith saw that her eyes were red. "So I sat down for a few minutes over there." She motioned to the fireplace. "I didn't mean to eavesdrop."

"Don't worry about it. You're probably sick of people asking, but how are you?"

"Holding myself together. Barely."

"This has to be so hard." Faith touched Nancy Z.'s arm. "Please let us know if there's anything we can do for you."

"Do you know the worst part? She'd been depressed lately. I tried to get her to open up about it. I just—" Nancy Z. wiped her cheek again. "So I'm trying to hold Vic together too, but he's a mess. He wanted to pack up and go. I don't know if I was right, but I got him to stay. I told him we can prop each other up and that we owe it to Nancy. He said he hasn't got the energy to leave anyway."

"Do you mind if I ask you something about the River Heights Roundtable?"

Nancy Z. waved her hand in dismissal. "It's gone. It's over. It wasn't really ever more than the two of us anyway."

"But can I ask if you two were playing pranks? Like tapping heels in the hallway late at night?"

"Games of cat and mouse." Nancy Z. laughed, then squeezed her eyes shut. "Rat and louse. Maybe we did, and maybe we didn't. But one thing we never did was let each other down. We never squealed."

Officer Jan Rooney called Faith back toward the end of the afternoon. "In answer to your question, it seems the officers who responded last night failed to secure a key fob for the car."

"Does that mean they had one or saw one, but now it's missing?" Faith asked.

"It appears there was a misstep. I take it there were a lot of spectators?"

"Yes, there were."

"That kind of confusion doesn't help," Officer Rooney said. "But as far as I can tell at this point, no key fob was found."

"I wonder why. Since the car has a keyless ignition, do you think it means someone took the fob while the car was running?"

"It means the Lighthouse Bay Police Department will continue investigating the incident," the officer said firmly.

"But at this point you'll be looking into it differently? As something possibly other than suicide or an accident?" Faith, mindful of Officer Rooney's professional responsibilities, rushed to add, "I don't expect you to tell me anything you can't or shouldn't, but everyone at the manor will want to cooperate in any way we can, and of course we have to consider our guests."

"We appreciate your willingness to cooperate, and we understand the situation at Castleton. But it would be premature to say anything more than we're continuing to look into the incident. Well, other than we'll want the fob you found."

"My cat deserves the credit."

"The one whose paw prints are on it."

Was that a glimmer of a sense of humor in cool Officer Rooney? Faith couldn't tell, but she hoped it was that rather than irritated resignation. "You'll need to come out to the manor to continue investigating the incident. But in the meantime, would you like me to drop off the fob at the station?"

"There's no need for you to make the trip. You were going to put the fob in a plastic bag. Did you do that?"

"Yes."

"Then hold on to it for now."

"It just raises so many questions—"

"Please hold on to those too," Officer Rooney interrupted. "We'll be in touch again soon. But right now Chief Garris needs to know what's happened, and his questions are going to be harder to answer than yours."

11

Faith wondered if she'd been terribly remiss in not telling Marlene about the fob when Watson discovered it. She also hadn't found out if the fob was a craft sample for the colloquium. But then why was it stuck in the dark corner of that cupboard? And what were the coins doing in there? There were so many questions.

Faith didn't think of herself as either particularly brave or cowardly, but she definitely felt the need to gather what courage she had before locking the library and heading down the stairs to Marlene's office.

Marlene's door was open, and Faith knocked on the frame, peeking around it the way Watson did when they played. And there was Watson, handsome as anything, sitting in one of the guest chairs in front of Marlene's desk.

He turned at Faith's knock and made happy cat eyes at her.

"Oh. Hello." Marlene sounded flustered, as though she'd been interrupted. "I'm not sure what your cat is doing. He does this sometimes. Comes in and sits here. I never know what he wants."

"I don't think he wants anything." Faith smiled. "I think he likes you."

"He does?"

Watson lifted his chin, as though agreeing, then jumped down and strolled out of the room.

"Well, what can I do for you? I'm quite busy," Marlene said. "The tours were a success, but they took more time than I'd anticipated."

"Officer Rooney called me—"

"Why you and not me?"

"The police will be calling you or stopping by soon. I'm sorry, but they're going to keep investigating Nancy A.'s death because of something Watson found this morning."

Marlene stared at her. "What did your cat find?"

She explained how Watson had discovered the key fob in the cupboard. "Nancy A. had one just like it. I don't know that the one Watson discovered is hers, but I called the police to see if they'd found hers. Officer Rooney called me back to say they hadn't. So now they're looking at the case differently."

"Looking at the case differently?" Marlene clucked her tongue. "There's a euphemism to write home about."

"She actually said, 'We're continuing to look into the incident.'"

"I think your euphemism gives a clearer picture than hers. And all this for a key fob the cat found in a cupboard?" Marlene frowned. "But they'll have to inspect the premises further. And you know what that means—more disruption."

"There could be a simple explanation for the missing fob. And Officer Rooney had a good question of her own—maybe one of the colloquium's crafts involves using the Nancy Drew silhouette. Perhaps they plan to apply the silhouette to key fobs, cell phones, luggage tags, and whatnot." Faith peered more closely at Marlene. "You've gone pale. Are you all right?"

"I just realized something," Marlene whispered. "That letter. We need to look at *it* differently now too."

"What do you mean?"

Marlene gazed at her desktop as though she'd just dropped the letter there. She pulled her hands back. "The letter was Nancy A.'s. She came to get it, but she said it was a joke. And the Nancies were jokers. You know that."

Faith nodded while her mind raced.

"Except on the sealed envelope she'd written, 'This is my insurance. In the event of my death, please open,'" Marlene went on. "And that doesn't sound like much of a joke right now."

"It doesn't, but what if it's part of a pattern? We still don't know how Bea's cat got in the passageways and Paloma heard heels tapping out Morse code outside her door Sunday night. What if the River Heights Roundtable arranged all of that?"

"You've raised good questions. I hope the letter is part of their Nancy Drew feud. But we're both thinking that's not the case. Am I correct?"

Faith nodded again, this time her mind firmly focused on the ramifications of the letter being genuine. "Where is the letter?"

"I don't think the police found it when they searched Nancy A.'s suite last night. If they had, they might have been looking at everything differently from the beginning." Marlene squared her shoulders. "This was a mistake. I need to call the police."

"It's an understandable mistake."

"I don't know if that's true. In any case, I'll let the police know about it. Here's another mistake. If this is murder, now I've made it easier for the murderer to sneak around and hide. I believe all the guests went on one of the passageway tours."

"You had no way of knowing," Faith reminded her. "And we still don't know."

Marlene sighed. "I'd better make that call."

The cat had enjoyed another delightful bonding session. He'd taken it upon himself to help the human discover and embrace her inner feline, and he felt she was making progress. She hardly jumped or squealed at all anymore when he surprised her in her underground lair, and sometimes she even gingerly stroked the top of his head.

When his human arrived, he left the two for their own tête-à-tête, and he embarked upon a sniffing tour to discover what savory or unsavory business might be apaw.

On her way back to the peace of the library, Faith thought about her own mistake—the missing map. But how was that a mistake? Using archival materials in a display was nothing out of the ordinary. The case was locked, and she was careful to lock the library when she left it. Nothing else was missing. *So how or who?*

Wolfe had been in the library when she'd arrived the day before. Maybe he'd taken it. Everything in the manor belonged to the Jaxons, and Wolfe had every right to take the map. If that was the case, then why didn't he mention it? She remembered their conversation and wondered if she'd rattled him so much that he'd forgotten to say anything. But she was fairly certain that librarians didn't rattle successful, international businessmen.

Then a thought struck: Was his joking a distraction so she wouldn't realize he had the map? She almost laughed at the outlandish notion.

Last night Faith had left a voice mail for Wolfe about Nancy A.'s death, and she hadn't heard from him. She hadn't seen him either. But that was not unusual, because of that successful, international businessman thing.

There was another possibility. Faith had insulted Marlene by asking if she'd borrowed the map for the tours. But what if one of the guests had managed to stay behind in the library when Marlene took a group into the passageways? It would be easy enough to do. Marlene wouldn't have expected it. Then that person could have rejoined the group at the end of the tour and left when Marlene unlocked the library door to let them out and the next group in.

Faith decided to take Marlene's advice about having more facts before accusing anyone else. And she knew just the women to help her get them—the members of the Candle House Book Club.

The book club usually met in the semicircle of cozy chairs in front of the huge stone fireplace in the Candle House Library in downtown Lighthouse Bay. The group read a wide variety of books and enjoyed one another's reviews, comments, and company. And Faith occasionally asked her friends for help in solving mysteries.

This evening all four members—Faith, Eileen, Midge, and Brooke—and two of their pets were in attendance. Watson rested in front of the fireplace, paws neatly tucked under his chin. Midge's Chihuahua, Atticus, was curled up on her lap.

"I've been thinking about everyone at Castleton today," Eileen said, taking her current knitting project out of her bag and getting to work. "Especially about the fiancé and the other Nancy. How are they coping? Are they even staying? I'm not sure I could."

"Nancy Z. said Vic doesn't have the energy to leave, but they're also staying to honor Nancy A. She said they're propping each other up." Faith paused. "But they might have another reason to stay."

"Does it involve the police?" Brooke asked. "Officer Tobin's car was parked in front of Nancy A.'s garage bay late this afternoon. The garage door was open about a foot. Like someone—maybe Officer Tobin—didn't like the idea of being in there with the door closed."

Faith pictured Officer Tobin, crawling all over the car and the garage, searching either methodically or madly for the missing key fob. "Official word from Officer Rooney is that they're continuing to look into the incident. She didn't say this, but it might not have been suicide or an accident."

The women were silent for a moment as they stared at one another, letting the news sink in.

Watson untucked himself and sat up straight.

"Does this have anything to do with a cat who's suddenly looking both interested and smug?" Midge asked.

"He's kind of a hero," Faith said, and she told them how Watson had discovered the key fob. "Officer Rooney suggested it might be a craft sample, but I keep forgetting to find out what crafts they're going to do this week."

"That information isn't on the website," Eileen said. "I checked earlier. I wanted to know what they were doing before I decide whether to go or not."

Faith made a note. "I'll ask and let you know. But there's more. It's a bunch of odd things that have happened. Maybe none of them are connected, or maybe some of them aren't really odd after all."

"Like what?" Brooke kicked her shoes off and pulled her feet up into the chair.

"There were tapping heels late at night in the hallway outside a guest's room," Faith answered.

"Tapping heels?" Midge repeated. "I want to hear more about that."

"I wish I had more to tell. Paloma heard them and wrote down the sequence of taps," Faith replied. "She showed it to Bea's son, Drew. He said it was Morse code, and he deciphered it for her. Except Bea says he doesn't know Morse code."

Eileen paused in her knitting. "What did the code say?"

"'SOS,' 'Beware,' and 'LOL.'"

"Someone goes in for funny Morse code," Brooke remarked. "Who else heard the tapping?"

"I don't know of anyone besides Paloma," Faith said.

"What if she didn't hear anything, but she's saying she did?" Midge suggested. "Maybe she's trying to add to the Nancy Drew atmosphere."

"Paloma called the tapping 'Drew extras' and asked me to thank the staff for providing them." Faith shrugged. "I guess she could be providing them herself."

"She'd have to be a good actress," Eileen said. "At dinner Sunday night, she and Bea both seemed genuinely surprised by the appearance of the letter."

"The mysterious letter Marlene received," Faith explained.

"What was in the letter?" Midge asked.

"That's a good question," Faith said. "And it's the kind of question that makes me glad you're all willing to take up book club time to help think this through. A sealed envelope was delivered to Marlene. We know what the note *on* it said: 'This is my insurance. In the event of my death, please open.' The note is signed 'Nancy.' But Marlene didn't open it, so we don't know what's in it."

"Or if there even is a letter," Midge said. "Tapping that no one else heard? A letter no one's seen?"

"Nancy A. went to pick up the letter yesterday," Faith said. "Marlene had put it in the safe. Nancy said it was hers and claimed it was a joke. Today Marlene wasn't so sure about it being a joke, and she called the police."

"Oh, speaking of mysteries, have you seen Bea's broken-heart locket?" Brooke asked. "You know me and romantic stories. I'm dying to ask who wears the other half." She cringed. "Although maybe under the circumstances, I shouldn't say dying."

"Faith did ask her," Eileen said, turning to her niece.

"I noticed that Bea touches the locket from time to time," Faith said, "so it seemed obvious that it means something to her and natural enough to ask her. But when I did, she said she prefers not to talk about it."

"See?" Brooke said, putting a hand over her heart. "It is romantic."

"There isn't anything odd about wearing a locket," Midge pointed out.

Faith glanced at Watson.

He'd resumed his tucked position, but he wasn't asleep. He blinked at her as if to say, *Go on. Tell them the rest.*

"There's even more," Faith continued. "There was the haunted staircase, which turned out to be Bea's cat that mysteriously got trapped behind the stairs, and now there's a map missing from the display case in the library."

"And don't forget the case of the skulking young man," Eileen said. "I told Midge about him—"

"But *I* don't know about him," Brooke interrupted.

"I saw Ned Carson, one of the colloquium guests, acting oddly outside Bea's suite Sunday night," Faith told her.

"And since then, I've heard reports that he's been seen around town," Midge said. "He's been spotted in Happy Tails and other places exhibiting the same unusual behavior. You can call it skulking, or you can call it searching. Either way, it's odd."

"But the latest might be even odder," Eileen said. "Ned came into Candle House and behaved like a normal library patron."

"Ooh, weird," Brooke teased.

"Smarty-pants," Eileen said with a laugh. "Here's the interesting part. When Seth was shelving books, he saw another young man who appeared to be following Ned." She turned to Faith. "What do you make of all this?"

"I don't know what to make of Ned. Or to be honest, any of it. I can't help but think the River Heights Roundtable was responsible for some of the pranks, though."

"*If* they're pranks," Eileen said.

"Exactly. I saw Nancy Z. this afternoon, and I asked her if they'd been playing around. I don't know if her answer was cryptic or just unhelpful. She said, 'Games of cat and mouse.' Then she laughed and said, '"Rat and louse. Maybe we did, and maybe we didn't. But one thing we never did was let each other down. We never squealed.'"

"I might understand the part about games of cat and mouse," Eileen said.

"That might be an admission," Midge suggested. "But the part about never letting each other down and never squealing sort of negates that."

"And what on earth does 'rat and louse' mean?" Brooke chimed in.

Faith shook her head. "About all I can tell you is that there's a whole lot of Nancy Drew going on."

When Faith arrived to unlock the library, she found Lois in the Great Hall Gallery, sitting on a plush chair brought from somewhere else, sipping tea and gazing out the French doors.

Faith smiled as she greeted her. "You certainly found a nice place to sit."

"I had my breakfast here too," Lois said. "It's much more pleasant."

"Really? More pleasant than what?"

"Than Bea buzzing angrily so that everyone knows how furious she is. Which she has every right to be, but I'm afraid my digestion also has rights." Lois leaned forward to look around Faith toward the lobby. "Oh dear. Here she comes again."

Faith heard the click of heels approaching rapidly from behind. *Do I want to know why Bea is so angry? Yes, I probably need to know.* She turned around with what she hoped was a pleasant, calm smile. "Good morning, Bea—"

"It is *not!*"

12

"My silver locket is gone." Bea crossed her arms over her chest. "It's not just missing. It. Is. Gone." Each of her words hit as hard as though she'd hammered it into the marble beneath their feet.

Lois got up, waved to Faith from behind Bea's back, and crept away.

"I am so sorry this has happened," Faith said. "Have you reported it to Marlene?"

"Of course I have," Bea snapped.

"Yes, I'm sure it was the first thing you did."

"And the first thing she did was tell me that the locks on guest suites are better than locks in most people's homes," Bea said. "The second thing she did was ask if I might have merely misplaced the locket. And I told her that I don't care how good the locks are. I don't care if the locks were forged for Fort Knox. My silver locket is gone. I stopped short of saying *stolen*. I could tell she did not want to hear that word."

Faith felt bad for Bea, but she also felt sorry for Marlene, who would not have intended to sound patronizing or defensive but might have come across that way to an angry guest.

Before Faith could respond, Bea started crying.

"Why don't you come into the library?" Faith asked gently. "No one else is there. Please come in, and let me see if I can help somehow."

From Bea's stiff posture, Faith sensed she was embarrassed about breaking down. She didn't reach a hand for Bea's shoulder or arm. Instead, she unlocked the library and led the way to the chairs in front of the fireplace.

"But I'm not going to sit, and I'm not going to take up your time." Bea sighed. "I'm a completely selfish and foolish old woman. It's childish to be so upset over a *thing*. For heaven's sake, Vic lost his fiancée, and

Nancy Z. lost her best friend, and they aren't throwing a tantrum. I'm just . . ." She held shaking hands up, palms out and fingers rigid.

"The locket might be a thing," Faith said, "but it means a lot to you. It isn't a trifle. Where did you keep it?"

"On the tall dresser in the suite. I always take the locket off at night. It's too delicate and precious to do otherwise."

"It's a beautiful piece of jewelry," Faith agreed. She thought a moment. "I don't know if Snowball is like this, but my cat enjoys pushing things off tables and shelves."

Bea almost smiled. "Snowball does too, but she can't jump that high anymore. I checked behind and under the dresser anyway—a dozen times. And I had Drew crawling over the entire floor, poor boy. But it's nowhere."

"Did the staff examine the lock and the door?"

"Yes, and they also checked every place Drew and I already looked. Then they kindly suggested that one of us might have left the room unlocked, which neither of us did." Bea drew in a sharp, tear-filled breath. "I'm not usually a pessimist, but I don't think I'll ever see the locket again."

Faith wondered if she would ever see the missing map again. She scrutinized the lock on the display case. It was intact, and, at least to her eye, it didn't appear tampered with.

She also checked to see if the map had miraculously reappeared in the case. It hadn't. It wasn't on the rolling cart, her desk, or a table or a chair. *And why would it be, because how did it get out of the case?*

She sighed and sent a text to Laura asking if she remembered seeing the map in the case. But Laura didn't have keys to the case or the library. She knew she should ask Wolfe too, but she needed time to figure out what to say and how to say it. *Accusing my employer—I do not want that on my to-do list.*

At some point it had started to rain. Faith turned on a few lamps to spill cozy light and counteract the gloom. Rainy days often brought more guests to the library, and that morning was no exception. Some came to gaze around and then left. Others brought a book with them or found one and settled into the chairs by the fireplace.

Nancy Z. came in and wandered over to the shelves, trailing her finger along one as though searching for a particular book. But while Faith watched, the trailing finger moved too randomly, and Nancy Z. never actually looked at the shelves or the books.

Faith didn't want to intrude, but she decided it wouldn't hurt to see if she could be of assistance. "Is there anything I can help you with?"

Nancy Z. stopped and smiled sadly at Faith. "Everyone here is so kind."

"I'm glad to hear that."

"Except . . ." Nancy Z. gazed beyond Faith to the other guests reading. "It's so quiet," she whispered. "I don't want to disturb anyone." She started trailing her finger again.

"Follow me. You won't disturb anyone in here." Faith escorted Nancy Z. into the small den off a corner of the library. It was like a private reading nook, and it was usually overlooked by guests who were dazzled by the rest of the library.

"I don't want to keep you," Nancy Z. said.

"You're not keeping me."

"I'm worried about Vic. He isn't himself. And I know, why would he be? I'm not myself either. But actually, I'm not sure if he's not himself, because I don't really know him."

"You don't?"

"It was a new relationship. Nancy and Vic. Well, newish."

"I see," Faith said. "So what worries you in particular?"

"A nasty conversation he had with Marlene about getting a refund for the unused portion of Nancy A.'s stay here. That Marlene is no doormat, is she?" Nancy Z. shrugged. "I don't know how to explain it. But Vic needs help. It's like he's stuck in a loop. He keeps telling the story of how they met at the auction and it was love at first sight."

"He told me that story the other day," Faith said.

"See? So then I wondered, was it love for each other or love for the car? And then I started wondering if it was love at all, because Vic didn't like to let either one of them out of his sight." Nancy Z. paused, then whispered, "Now I'll never see her again. And neither will he."

For the second time that morning, Faith heard about something or someone lost and never to be seen again. Like a lamentation, the sad refrain suited the gloomy day.

Lois entered the library shortly before lunch with an invitation for Faith. "I wondered if you'd like to join me in town for lunch at one of those cute little places."

"I would love to—"

"But you already have plans?" Lois broke in.

"It won't be nearly as tasty as yours. It's a quick working lunch for me. I've spent too much time playing this week."

"Which reminds me. You missed most of the excitement during that panel discussion. Why don't you see if you can get ahold of the video they made. Sparks were flying."

And only hours later, Nancy A. was dead. "Thanks. I'll look into it."

After her peanut butter sandwich, Faith called the tech guy she'd seen setting up the two cameras for the panel discussion Monday afternoon.

"I can't send the files to you," he told her. "The recordings belong to that group. You'll have to talk to them."

She made a note to ask Bea and Paloma for permission to watch the video the next time she saw them.

Then she called the police station, and when she was connected to Officer Rooney, she mentioned the video and Lois's remark about sparks flying.

"That's certainly interesting."

"Isn't it? Lois is a sweet old lady who enjoys watching real-life drama, and she thinks I do too."

"And what's your point in telling me about the video?" the officer asked.

"I thought that something could have happened during the panel discussion that led to Nancy A.'s death. Maybe you would want to see the video for that reason. For evidence."

"Has your friend told you about any particular incident that happened during the panel discussion?"

"No."

"Then without a specific reason for thinking the interactions during that panel discussion hold useful information, I'll have to decline. It's not that I don't like real-life drama, but it wouldn't be the best use of my time, if you see what I mean."

Faith appreciated Officer Rooney's nicely phrased professional brush-off. "I still have the key fob. Did Officer Tobin find anything in the car or the garage bay when he was here yesterday?"

"I'll stop by the library and pick up the fob while I'm at the manor this afternoon."

A sidestep this time instead of a brush-off. "You'll be here looking for the letter?"

There was a pause, and Faith pictured the officer rolling her eyes before asking, "What do you know about a letter?"

Faith told Officer Rooney the little she knew about the letter. Then she described the scene at the dinner when she noticed Nancy A. leave the room and also the various pranks. "If that's what they are.

For instance, we don't know if there's really a letter inside the envelope. It could be blank paper."

"I'll stop by later this afternoon." Officer Rooney hung up.

When Officer Rooney arrived at the manor, she didn't offer any more information than she had on the phone. She didn't encourage questions either. She took the key fob from Faith, thanked her, and walked out.

Faith was left feeling flat. "Not that I thought she *needed* to confide in me," she said to Watson. "But we have been helpful in the past."

Shortly after Officer Rooney left the library, Brooke and Lois entered and ganged up on Faith. They lured her to the coffee and gift shop at the opposite end of the manor—Lois with bright eyes and Brooke with a napkin-covered tray. It hadn't taken much more than the buttery, chocolaty scent of that tray to get Faith to lock the library and follow.

Iris Alden, who managed the coffee and gift shop, brought three cups of coffee and cheerful greetings to the table they took in the corner. She happily accepted a chocolate croissant Brooke offered her, then returned to the counter.

As soon as Iris was gone, Brooke turned to Faith. "Okay, spill it. Lois noticed Officer Rooney arrive and head for the offices in the basement. Then we both saw her going to the library. What did you learn?"

"Promise you won't take my croissant away if I disappoint you?" Faith pulled her pastry closer. "Officer Rooney came to get the fob, but that's all I know at this point. She didn't tell me anything, and she isn't interested in our input. I think it's only so much useless trivia to her."

"That sounds shortsighted," Lois commented. "In my experience, one woman's bit of useless trivia is another woman's revealing detail. I think you should stay focused and keep in mind those three small words *at this point*."

"Sifting the useless information from the useful is the trick," Faith said. "I wonder—"

"Look at her." Brooke motioned to Faith. "You can see the wheels turning. That's the sign of a serious sifter."

Lois nodded. "After all, she is a librarian."

"What would you think of having another book club meeting tonight?" Faith asked.

Brooke turned to Lois and grinned. "By 'book club,' she means part-time sleuth support team."

"We can meet at my place," Faith went on, "and I'll make supper. Lois, you're invited too. You can be an honorary member. We can use your help in making sense of all this."

"I have another suggestion," Lois said. "After supper, why don't you all join us for the Nancy Drew Trivia Night? As you can imagine, the colloquium is operating under a cloud, and we're all looking forward to some fun."

"That's a good idea," Faith replied. "One woman's bit of fun might be another woman's seemingly trivial but revealing detail."

The cat had not followed his human when she was greeted by the other two. The tray carried by one of the humans did not entice him. He'd noticed that her skill at carrying trays with mouthwatering aromas was haphazard. Sometimes a tray would smell delightfully of salmon or shrimp, but other times the aroma wasn't interesting at all. He preferred to ignore her failures.

When he turned the corner, he spied the nice human from the top floor of the manor loping toward the library. With stealth and cunning, the cat tracked the person and watched him unlock the door. This required looking into.

But to catch a debonair person, a handsome cat should be properly attired. He stopped to tidy his tuxedo, raising his hind leg like a flag, signaling that here was not only a natty dresser but also a thorough and conscientious cat.

The cat often found that attending to one area led to polishing and straightening three or four more areas—paws, whiskers, ears, the paws again—a labor of love requiring deepest concentration.

Upon finishing, he glistened his way to the library door and peered around it at his prey, only to find that the nice human had cornered his own prey.

Faith caught Watson peeking around the edge of the library door. *So you think you're sneaking up on me, do you? Wait. Why is the door open?*

Watson must have heard her approach. He glanced at her, then went back to peering around the door.

She took her cue from him and slowed to a tiptoe. Just when she was within a whisker of poking her head through the doorway, she heard raised male voices in the library.

"No, that's not what I was doing."

"Then tell me what you *were* doing."

The first voice she couldn't identify, but the second, sounding much angrier because it was low and controlled, was Wolfe's.

Faith took a steadying breath and walked in. "Good afternoon, gentlemen. Is everything all right?"

Ned Carson, his back pressed against the bookshelves, faced a looming Wolfe Jaxon, all the more menacing for his tailored three-piece suit. Neither of them shifted position at Faith's greeting.

"I found him taking books off the shelves one by one," Wolfe said. "He was flipping through them, obviously searching for something tucked inside. His actions are somewhat suspicious, don't you think?"

"Not just somewhat, and that isn't the half of it." Faith mentioned Ned's peculiar behavior of skulking in the manor's corridors and around Lighthouse Bay in his crepe-soled shoes. "There are two more things, and maybe you know something about them too." She faced Ned. "Bea Stapleton's locket is missing from her room. Have you heard about that?"

Ned's gaze flicked left, and then he blinked and gazed at her again. "Bea let everyone know about it at breakfast."

"And a map is missing from the display case," Faith continued. "Did you take it?"

"What?" Ned said. "No."

"But right now, the biggest question is, how did you get in here?" Faith asked. "The door was locked."

Ned pointed at Wolfe. "He unlocked the door, and I followed him in. He went left. I went right. Can I help it if my skulking is better than his hearing?"

"You're in no position to make jokes," Wolfe said. "And I suggest you tell us exactly what you have been doing."

"Who's asking?"

Faith was surprised at Ned's cocky question, considering Wolfe still loomed over him. "Wolfe, this is Ned Carson, one of our colloquium guests. Ned, this is Wolfe Jaxon, co-owner of Castleton Manor."

"Hey, my apologies, man." Ned put his hands together and brought them up to rest against his lips.

Not so much in a plea but as if he needs to blow on them to warm them, Faith thought.

"I haven't done anything wrong, and I haven't meant any harm.

Honest." Ned shrugged, then tucked his hands into his armpits. "I've been following the clues in a letter my father left me."

Wolfe cocked his head. "Clues?"

"It sounds crazy, right? Believe me, it feels crazy. A year ago, Dad was diagnosed with a terminal cancer, which he didn't take seriously. He always said he knew only two things for certain—that you should believe in yourself and that you should question authority. And when he'd say that, I was always the smart-aleck kid, and I'd say I had questions about that second thing. He died six weeks ago."

"You have my sympathies," Wolfe said.

"I'm sorry for your loss." Faith's heart went out to Ned, but she still wondered about his explanation. "What's the connection with the manor? You haven't told us what you're doing here."

"To be honest, I'm not entirely sure what I'm doing here," Ned admitted. "But according to his letter, Dad finally accepted that he was dying, and he visited Lighthouse Bay and Castleton Manor. That must have been six months ago. Dad was a game designer, and he created a treasure hunt of sorts for me. At the end he wrote, 'All will be revealed.' He paid my registration for the colloquium. I didn't know about any of this until his lawyer sent the letter to me after Dad died."

"That's quite a . . . story." Faith knew she sounded skeptical. "So leafing through the books and skulking around are—"

"Following clues," Ned finished.

"Are you really a graduate student?" she asked.

"Oh yeah. Absolutely. I'm writing my master's thesis on the Stratemeyer Syndicate, so the colloquium fits right in. I haven't figured out why Dad chose this place or this event for the treasure hunt, other than the expediency of killing two birds with one stone, but maybe I'll find that out too."

Watson ambled over and sniffed at the men's pant legs. He rubbed his jaw against Ned's shin.

He probably wishes he'd say more about birds, Faith thought.

"This is fascinating," Wolfe said, leaning a shoulder against the bookshelves. "Do you want help with the clues so you can finish the game sooner or skip ahead?"

Ned shook his head emphatically. "I'm not questioning my dad this time. This was the last game he designed. I'm going to honor him and see it through. I need to do that."

"That's completely understandable," Wolfe said.

"May I have your permission to keep working on this clue?"

"Yes, of course," Wolfe replied.

Ned thanked him, then went back to flipping through books.

Faith and Wolfe moved over to the display case.

"Do you believe him?" Faith whispered.

"I'm willing to give him the benefit of the doubt," Wolfe answered. "Basic facts of his story are easy enough to check out. I'm more interested in the missing map."

"I am so sorry about that," Faith rushed to say. "I was sure the case was locked—"

Wolfe stopped her with a wave of his hand. "When Marlene told me about the map, I came to see if you'd had it in the case I remembered. It's a lovely antique, and it's been in the family for generations. However, the lock is capable of being picked by a seven-year-old with a hairpin or a paper clip. This is not your fault."

Faith frowned. "But the map is still missing."

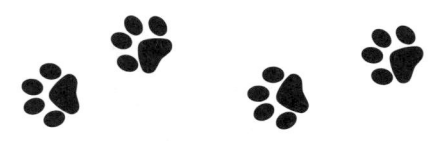

Toward the end of the afternoon, Faith was passing through the Great Hall Gallery when her phone buzzed with a text from Eileen. She slowed to read it, then paused in front of the statue of Agatha Christie to compose an answer. As she hit send, she nearly dropped her phone.

The statue of Agatha Christie had just whispered, "Please come to me."

13

Agatha Christie did not just ask me to come to her, Faith told herself.

She glanced around and was startled to find Paloma on her hands and knees in the niche behind the statue. "Paloma, are you all right?"

Paloma stared up at Faith without saying a word.

"Did I hear you correctly?" Faith asked.

Paloma laughed and got to her feet, dusting off her knees.

Knowing how conscientious the Castleton maintenance staff was, Faith doubted that Paloma's knees needed dusting. She also doubted the woman's laugh.

"You heard that?" Paloma finally replied. "It was only a joke." She laughed again.

But Faith saw worry and something else in her eyes. *Desperation?* "Are you sure? If there's something going on or if there's anything I can do for you, please let me know."

"No. I mean, I will let you know if I do need something. See you later." And Paloma practically ran to get away.

In Faith's experience, the Lighthouse Bay Police Department operated efficiently, carefully, and as discreetly as they could while still being thorough. Except for Officer Rooney stopping by the library for the key fob, she was barely aware of their presence at the manor that afternoon.

But Marlene's experience was clearly much different. "Another nightmare," she grumbled when she bumped into Faith before leaving at the end of the day. "Poking, prying, asking questions, disturbing, disrupting, upsetting."

"Did the officers upset the guests?" Faith asked. "Did you have a lot of complaints to deal with?"

"I'm not talking about the guests," Marlene said. "*I* was upset. They disrupted *me*. The guests are off in their own Nancy Drew la-la land. Some of them even believed the police were part of the so-called extras we planned. They thought it was entertainment. There are no extras, except for the extra-large headache all this is giving me."

"Go home and kick back. You deserve some rest."

Marlene nodded. "I thought about attending their trivia night, but a quiet evening with a movie and my friend the popcorn bowl sounds much more appealing."

Faith fixed one of her favorite simple meals for a crowd—a crisp green salad and cheese tortellini with fresh tomatoes, olives, and artichoke hearts tossed with olive oil, plenty of basil, and oregano. She added enough garlic to wake it up but not so much that any of them would scare people later at trivia night.

As she cooked she felt like a fashionable chef from the 1930s. For the dress-up trivia night, she'd decided to wear Great-Grandmother Florry's high-waisted, wide-legged trousers. She'd put the magnifying glass from the colloquium tote in her trouser pocket as a fun accessory.

"What do you think, Watson?" she said, taking off her apron. "Does it look tasty enough to pass muster with Brooke and healthy enough to suit Midge and Aunt Eileen?"

Watson meowed as if in agreement.

The doorbell rang, and Faith rushed to open the door.

"The trousers!" Eileen exclaimed. "They're perfect."

"You don't look too shabby yourself."

"It's literally an old thing I haven't worn in years," Eileen said. "But I'm sure someone somewhere has said that plaid jumpers never go out of style."

"You must have inherited Florry's gene for thrift and saving," Faith teased.

"Some people call it hoarding," Eileen retorted. "What help do you need in the kitchen?"

"Just plates and glasses."

"Then I'll get those," Eileen volunteered as the doorbell rang. "You go answer that."

Faith opened the door to Midge, Brooke, and Lois. The three newcomers were clad in outfits honoring the girl sleuth. Midge wore a skirt and twinset with a strand of pearls, Brooke had on a trench coat, and Lois sported a fedora and carried a knitting bag.

Faith flipped her shirt collar up and stood for a moment in the Katharine Hepburn pose she'd been practicing. She said in a decent Hepburn imitation, "I do so want you to come in. Really I do."

The trio laughed.

"I brought dessert," Brooke announced, holding up a covered plate. "Apple crumble cheesecake."

"It sounds delicious," Faith said. "Thank you."

After Faith ushered them inside, they joined Eileen in the kitchen. The women helped themselves to the food and settled in the living room, balancing plates on their knees.

Watson, obviously not interested in pasta or salad, retreated to his post on the back of the sofa.

The women chatted while they ate, and Faith turned to Lois during a lull in the conversation. "I just realized that I don't know your last name."

"It's Gruen."

"No," Brooke said. "Like Hannah? Really?"

Lois smiled. "No, not really. But wouldn't that be fun? It's close, though. It's Gruenwald."

"Besides the fact that you love the Castleton library and seem to be a keen student of human nature," Faith said, "I'm afraid I can't tell the others much about you."

"Is that a 'keen' student or a 'Keene' student?" Midge asked, holding up a magnifying glass.

The women laughed.

"Your knitting bag tells me an important thing about you." Eileen motioned to the bag at Lois's feet. "My bag is in the car, and it's coming with me to trivia night. My little gray cells engage better with needles in my hands."

"Mine too," Lois agreed. "I'm so happy to be staying at Castleton. I've had a hankering to visit for years, and this colloquium seemed like the perfect opportunity to indulge myself. As for my knitting and love for books, I come by them naturally, but they were also my career. For thirty years, I owned a book and yarn shop in Chelmsford called Yarns and Yarns."

"Oh, I love the name," Brooke commented.

"We had a book club at the shop too, which is one of the things I miss, so thank you for welcoming me to yours." Lois smiled at the other women, her eyes shining. "But our book club didn't have a sideline in amateur sleuth support."

"Speaking of sleuthing . . ." Faith set her empty plate aside and picked up the notebook she'd written in Monday night. "Let me tell you the latest developments concerning furtive Ned, the missing map and the lost locket, a whispering statue, and now not one but *two* mysterious letters. And I don't mean any of that to sound frivolous next to Nancy A.'s death."

"Is her death officially considered questionable now?" Midge asked. "I heard about the police being at the manor again this afternoon. Let's start with that."

"I haven't heard anything official," Faith said.

"Which she finds very frustrating," Brooke added.

"But at least unofficially, there seem to be questions," Midge said. "Thanks to Watson's key fob. Although I have to say, calling it an accident never felt right to me. Sitting in a running car in a closed garage? It seems like she would have known better."

"Officer Tobin said the same thing that night," Faith replied. "And there are people who don't believe it could be suicide, but that's not unusual in these cases. So, yes, the key fob and the envelope were enough to bring the police back out, and I'm frustrated that Officer Rooney doesn't see fit to send me daily briefings on their cases."

"The least she could do is send the briefings to Watson," Brooke said.

Faith grinned. "Exactly."

"Why don't I text her and suggest that?" Brooke pulled her phone out.

Everyone laughed.

"This is why all of you are good for me," Faith said. "You make me laugh, but you also listen."

"So tell us about the second mysterious letter and nefarious Ned," Eileen said.

"Those two are actually connected, but let me talk about the whispering statue first, because it's Drewian and completely weird." Faith told them about hearing the whisper and finding Paloma on her hands and knees behind the Agatha Christie statue. "That's an example of something odd that Officer Rooney wouldn't want to hear."

"You can hardly blame her," Eileen said. "What in heaven's name was Paloma doing?"

"I have no idea. She told me it was a joke, and then she could hardly scurry away fast enough. Ned, on the other hand, told us exactly what he's been doing." Faith related that part of her afternoon, pausing only when Brooke retrieved the apple crumble cheesecake and passed around slices to the others.

They were silent for a few minutes as they savored the scrumptious dessert.

Midge spoke up first. "Ned's the obvious suspect."

"For Nancy A.'s death?" Brooke asked. "Why?"

"That's a sketchy story, his behavior has been sketchy all along, and he had opportunity," Midge explained.

"I mean, why would he kill her?" Brooke asked.

"I don't know. That's what investigations are for," Midge answered. "Especially police investigations. And I can't believe they didn't look for car keys that night."

"That's one thing Officer Rooney did let slip," Faith said. "She said Chief Garris would have a few questions about that error too."

"Bryan Laddy's young," Eileen said.

"But he's still a police officer," Midge retorted.

"Seeing Nancy A. like that was a horrible experience," Faith said quietly. She opened her notebook to a fresh page and wrote Ned's name under the word *Suspects*.

"Point taken," Midge said. "I wasn't in Laddy's shoes, and even though I have medical experience, I might have been rattled too. Besides, if they'd found keys, the killer would be getting away with this. But I still say it's Ned."

"But if Ned killed Nancy A., then why did he take a chance on 'discovering' her?" Brooke asked. "It put him in the wrong place at the wrong time, and it made him *look* like the obvious suspect. Doesn't that clear him?"

"Or it gave him a convenient story," Midge suggested. "Like his story this afternoon."

Wolfe had said the basics of Ned's story would be easy enough to check. Faith put a check mark next to Ned's name where she'd written it. "Why would he—or anyone—take the key fob and hide it in a cupboard? Why not get rid of it?"

"That's the kind of question that must drive Jan Rooney crazy,"

Eileen remarked. "What about this letter from Ned's father? Do you believe him, Faith? Did he show it to you?"

"I guess we could ask him to." Faith made another quick note. "I'm not sure I do believe the story."

"See?" Midge piped up. "He is suspicious."

"Wolfe believes him," Faith said.

"I believe him," Lois said.

"You've probably seen him more than some of us," Eileen said, turning to Lois. "So why do you believe him?"

"I like his shoes," Lois stated. "They look trustworthy, possibly because my nephew wears shoes like that. He says they have good soles, and he's a good soul."

"That's a very Miss Marple observation," Eileen said.

Lois smiled. "Isn't it? I must be channeling her this evening."

"Even if Ned's story is true, it doesn't mean he's innocent," Faith reminded them. "But there's also Vic Flynn, Nancy A.'s fiancé."

"Is he still at Castleton?" Eileen said. "Did the police ask him to stay?"

"I'm not sure they did initially," Faith replied, "but they might have at this point."

"He seems to just be going through the motions of participating in colloquium events," Lois said. "Although to be honest, I'm not sure that's much of a change. From the beginning, he's been more of a plus-one than a true Drew fan. And if I'm honest to the point of sounding like Bea, he isn't really Drew material."

"I think Nancy Z. has kind of taken him under her wing," Brooke observed.

"That's probably good for him and good for her too," Midge said.

"At least he knows someone at this sad time. The group is a sea of strangers to him," Lois told them. "Did you know that Vic and Nancy A. met over that wonderful car? I'm not sure how I would feel about a car after something like this happened."

"Nancy Z. isn't sure how Vic feels either," Faith said. "But she's beginning to wonder who he loved more—Nancy A. or the car."

"That's the kind of detail that really ought to interest the police." Eileen pointed at Faith's notebook. "Be sure you write that down."

"Nancy Z. told me she doesn't really know Vic, though. She said it was a new relationship. Oh—" Faith stopped, remembering where her game of tailing with Watson had ended up Monday morning. "I overheard an argument about money between Nancy A. and Vic. He was complaining about the expense of being here and called it fantasizing. She asked him why he'd come. He said maybe he should go—" She stopped again.

Eileen studied her face. "What else did they say?"

"She said, 'See if I care.' And he said, 'You will.'" Faith made another note and looked up as she realized the others had gone quiet. "Vic left the room after saying that, and then Nancy A. left too."

Lois shook her head. "That doesn't bode well for Vic."

"Did anything else happen?" Brooke asked Faith.

"That afternoon, when Nancy A. was going to give me a ride in the roadster, she sent Vic inside to get her sweater. As soon as he was out of sight, she told me to hop in and we took off. She talked about escape."

"Couples argue, especially if there are money problems," Midge pointed out. "But I'll concede that money problems might also lead to motives."

"Do we want to know where you were that you overheard that argument?" Brooke asked.

"Let me just say it's an experience I'd rather not repeat." Faith glanced at Watson who'd been observing from the back of the sofa.

The cat sat up, yawned ostentatiously, and turned his back on the room to gaze out the window.

The others were quiet again until Lois turned to Faith and said, "You were going to tell them about Bea's lost locket."

"The locket," Brooke echoed. "It's beautiful. I'm sorry it's missing.

But even I, with my romantic soul, know when someone is carrying on too far. At breakfast this morning, Bea ranted about it to everyone. The other guests were so uncomfortable that they walked out in a hurry, leaving a truly awful amount of food on their plates."

"Missing, presumed stolen," Faith told Eileen and Midge. "One more Drewian mystery. It disappeared out of Bea's suite overnight."

"Her cat supposedly disappeared out of her suite too," Eileen said. "Have you heard any more about how that happened?"

Faith shook her head.

"From what I saw of Bea, she's very much in charge," Eileen commented. "Or at least she expects to be."

Lois nodded. "She's very much in charge of that poor son of hers too."

"Why do you call him a poor son?" Brooke asked.

"His name, if nothing else," Lois answered. "Drew is a perfectly good name but not in this situation. Why on earth did she torture him that way?"

"You'd rather she'd chosen another way?" Brooke asked. "Sorry, bad joke."

"On the contrary," Lois said. "I think she finds a number of ways to make him unhappy. But she's sure of herself, and she's probably sure she knows what's best for him. Just as she knows what's best for her other child—her beloved Nancy Drew Clue Society."

"She was very kind to Nancy Z. the night Nancy A. died," Faith said.

"She took charge of her, but I don't know what it means," Lois admitted. "I don't *know* that it was kindness."

"They did have that rivalry going," Midge said. "When the two Nancies came into Snickerdoodles on Monday, they could hardly contain themselves."

"Paloma's not exactly a peace dove either," Faith said. "She has an almost visceral reaction to the Nancies, and she makes it easy for them to get to her. She has huge buttons, and the Nancies don't just push them—they jump on them and do the jitterbug."

"Maybe that's why she was on her hands and knees whispering behind a statue," Midge suggested. "Perhaps she's cracking under the pressure. I mean that seriously."

"If she's hurting, then someone should keep an eye on her," Lois said. Eileen raised her eyebrows. "Or if she's hurt someone else."

"Oh yes, I see," Lois remarked. "This must be where the sleuth support services come in. How does that work?"

"Largely self-directed." Eileen stood and started gathering empty plates and glasses. "I'll see what I can find out about Vic and Ned online. Well, the others too. Why not?"

"Let's try to keep an eye on Paloma and engage the others in conversation more often," Faith added. "Starting soon at Nancy Drew Trivia Night. Does everyone have her magnifying glass?"

The cat escorted the humans through the dark. It wasn't really dark. Not total darkness. Not as totally black as the fire pit on the beach. He lifted his paws higher and shook them at the memory of cold waves. Water told him only one thing—wet. Fire was more interesting, more nuanced, more feline. Like a cat, fire was sometimes warm, sometimes licking, sometimes striking with savage spitting and ferocious leaps. And sometimes fire left behind intriguing smells.

The cat sat on a balustrade, watching to be sure the cold moonlight on the tiled loggia didn't wash over the humans and swallow them up.

When they reached the door safely, he jumped down and followed the path to the beach where he could refresh his memory of the curling scents of charred wood and paper.

14

Nancy Drew Trivia Night was set up in the Great Hall Gallery. When Faith, Eileen, Brooke, Midge, and Lois arrived, they found Bea and Paloma huddled in a private conversation behind the registration table, which was set up in front of the statue of Agatha Christie. By far, Agatha appeared to be the calmest of the three.

Bea and Paloma were so intent on their conversation that they didn't notice the book club members approaching.

"I merely want to remind people that the locket is still missing," Bea said. "I see nothing wrong with that."

"They feel as though you're accusing them," Paloma told her.

"They're right. I am accusing *someone*, because someone is responsible. Someone knows where the locket is, knows who took it, or knows how it was taken. It's as simple as that."

"But most of them don't know, and some of them still think it might show up misplaced—"

"And they are *wrong*," Bea interrupted.

Paloma turned and noticed Faith and her friends. "Oh, look," she said with a sudden false cheer in her voice, "here are five more players to register. Wonderful. You can have three per team."

"We didn't think about teams." Faith glanced around and saw trios scattered around the room, heads together. *Planning strategy? We didn't think about that either.* Then she realized they had—just a different kind of strategy. "Do you have groups that need thirds? We can fill those out."

Paloma picked up a clipboard and checked her list. "Perfect. We have five teams that need another player." She beckoned, and Faith and the others leaned closer. "But I must warn you. No one wants to join the Rambunctious Roadsters." She gestured to a table where Nancy Z. and Vic sat alone.

"Too depressing?" Faith asked.

"It takes the competitive edge off," Paloma replied. "People are here to win. Haven't you heard our battle cry?"

"Battle cry?" Midge repeated.

"Be Drew or Die."

"I'll join the Roadsters," Faith volunteered.

"*Rambunctious* Roadsters." Paloma made a check mark on the list. Then she assigned Eileen to the Sleuthsayers, Midge to the Girl Gumshoes, Brooke to the Diva Detectives, and Lois to the Clue Busters. "Good luck." She hurried away.

"This might not work out exactly the way we'd hoped," Eileen whispered to Faith, "and I seriously doubt that I'll be an asset to my team."

"I doubt any of us will be, except for Lois. But you know what they say."

"Be gracious in defeat?"

"Be Drew or Die."

"That strikes me as very poor taste under the circumstances."

At seven o'clock sharp, Bea called the teams to order. Faith and the others rushed to join their teams. Bea introduced herself as the trivia master and Paloma as scorekeeper, then explained the rules of the game.

All the teams—except for the Rambunctious Roadsters—cheered the news that prizes would be awarded at the end of the evening, and they cheered again when Bea told them a break for refreshments would occur at the halfway point.

The Rambunctious Roadsters appeared to be running on tires with slow leaks, and every team they squared off against had a winning round and left the table happy. Faith didn't mind, as she was having an interesting conversation with Nancy Z., albeit in sixty-second snatches.

Vic actually showed some interest in answering the questions Bea called out. He was on his own for most of them, though, because every question reminded Nancy Z. of something she and Nancy A. had done together.

"We always said we'd do anything for each other," Nancy Z. told Faith in response to a question about the names of Nancy Drew's sleuthing friends.

When Bea asked what job Henry Winch did in *The Clue of the Broken Locket*, Nancy Z. remarked, "She paid my way here when I lost my job. I'd have done the same for her in a heartbeat."

When asked where Ned Nickerson attended college, Nancy Z. said, "*She* was a great student. She should have stuck it out, gone for the doctorate somewhere else if she had to."

"What do you mean?" Faith asked her.

Vic crumpled up their answer sheet. "Nancy was her student." He jerked his thumb over his shoulder.

"Bea's?" Faith asked.

"They agreed to disagree," Vic said, "and Nancy left the program. Water under the bridge and long gone. She had a good job. She was happier and better off out of there, and she knew it."

Faith looked at Nancy Z.

"Vic wasn't in the picture yet," Nancy Z. explained. "But he's right about everything except agreeing to disagree. There were a lot of tears back then."

"I'm not sure I ever heard what Nancy did for a living," Faith said.

"Investment banker." Vic rubbed his fingertips together. "A good one."

"And what about you?" Faith asked Nancy Z. "I'm sorry about the job. What was it?"

"Goldie's loss, that's what it was. His loss."

Faith didn't press her further.

Halfway through the contest, Bea announced the break for refreshments. The Passionfruit Password Punch and cookies shaped like magnifying glasses and skeleton keys were a hit.

The break from the game gave Faith and her friends a chance to compare notes.

"Who knew," Eileen said, "but the Sleuthsayers are slaying the competition."

"The Diva Detectives aren't doing too badly either," Brooke said. "How are the Roadsters?"

"Less than rambunctious from what I could tell during our round with them," Lois remarked.

"Off the road and in the ditch," Midge added.

"Laugh all you like," Faith said, glancing around to see if anyone was within earshot. No one was, but she lowered her voice anyway. "We're losing because I've been grilling the suspects and gathering information." She turned to Lois. "Do you remember that first afternoon at the registration table when I asked Bea and Paloma if they'd met the Nancies before?"

"Yes, and Paloma was quite agitated about them and what they might do."

"Vic and Nancy Z. just told me that Nancy A. was one of Bea's graduate students once upon a time. But that afternoon, when I asked Bea if she'd met the Nancies, Bea shook her head."

Faith looked for Watson before starting home. He seemed to like being out on moonlit nights. But there was no sign of him.

Eileen offered to help her with the dishes, but Faith shooed her aunt home.

She washed up and then sat with her notebook and laptop.

Much later, she heard a familiar meow outside. "Are you home from the sea, my wanderer?" she asked as she opened the door.

Watson brushed her leg as he came in, then stretched his paws far out in front of him and yawned.

Faith yawned too. "It's contagious. But it's a good idea. What do you say, time for bed?"

The next morning Faith walked to the manor with Watson at her heels. As soon as they walked through the door, Watson took off.

Faith joined Eileen and Lois in the crafts room for the colloquium's craft and coffee event. They served themselves coffee and sat down at one of the tables.

"I had no idea the competition would be so cutthroat during the trivia game last night," Lois commented. "And people were so serious about it all. It was enjoyable, though."

"For those who won," Faith teased.

"And weren't the prizes generous?" Lois continued. "Imagine my surprise, winning a fifty-dollar gift certificate to the bookstore of my choice."

"You certainly deserved it," Eileen said as she set her knitting bag on the table. "You helped the Clue Busters finish in first place."

"Why the knitting today?" Lois asked. "Aren't you making the craft?"

"Yes, but this is show-and-tell," Eileen responded. "And an advertisement. I'm finishing a cardigan inspired by Nancy Drew for a silent auction we're holding at the library. It's a fund-raiser for a local literacy foundation."

Nancy Z. walked in with two other women. They took their seats at Faith's table.

Vic stuck his head in and then quickly disappeared. The women coming in behind him laughed and said he'd practically run over them to get away.

"Who's demonstrating?" one of the women asked.

"Me," Paloma said, striding through the door. "I hope I didn't keep you waiting."

"Not at all," Lois said.

"Good. Here's what we're making this morning." Paloma walked around the tables, showing the women the necklace she was wearing—a simple beaded strand with a large, clear glass cabochon as the centerpiece. Magnified from behind the cabochon was the classic Nancy Drew silhouette.

Eileen smiled. "It will make a wonderful gift for my granddaughter."

"You'll find everything you need in front of you," Paloma went on. "But feel free to move around and look at the beads on the other tables. This craft is all about getting your creative juices going and spending time together. No mysteries involved. Any questions?"

"I can think of a mystery," a woman sitting across from Faith said. "How do I decide which beads to choose first?"

"Easy," Paloma answered. "Just close your eyes."

The room became quiet as the women got down to work, planning and choosing and threading. There was an ample supply of materials, tools, and hardware, including a variety of Nancy Drew artwork to pair with the cabochons. As they settled in and started stringing their beads, conversations started again.

"Bea isn't a crafter?" Faith asked when Paloma stopped at their table.

"Bea enjoys knitting. She wanted to attend, but she has an appointment with Marlene about her missing locket. The poor thing."

Faith thought "poor thing" could apply to either Bea or Marlene.

"Knitting is such a calm and meditative craft," Lois said. "Show us the Nancy Drew cardigan for the silent auction, Eileen."

Eileen removed the sweater from her bag and held it up.

"Beautiful," a woman gushed. "I had a cat that same soft gray. Her name was Purrl with two *r*'s."

"How's the auction coming, Aunt Eileen?" Faith asked.

"There's a lot more work to do." Eileen tucked the knitting back into her bag and squinted at her beads. "Thank goodness for volunteers. But it's not nearly as much work as putting together something like this colloquium. I don't know how you do it, Paloma."

"She stepped out," a woman at the next table said. "She'll be back in a few."

Eileen laughed. "That's what happens when I get going on a project like this. Tunnel vision. How many volunteers are involved in the colloquium?"

"Are there any?" the woman next to her asked.

"I think so," Faith answered. "Paloma told me volunteers do all the work."

"*They're* the volunteers," Nancy Z. said. "The bee and the bird."

"Paloma's the behind-the-scenes organizer," the woman next to Eileen stated. "She arranges the program schedule, puts together the goody bags, writes the newsletters, and all of that. But she does it with Bea's vision. Bea is the heart and soul. Without her, there wouldn't be a Nancy Drew Clue Society or the Nancy Drew Clue Colloquium."

"It's true," Nancy Z. admitted. "As much as Nancy A. and I liked to razz Bea, I admire her."

"She accomplished a great deal over the span of her career," another woman said. "If she put her mind to it, she got it done."

Nancy Z. nodded. "I'm pretty sure Bea is capable of anything."

"What do you mean by 'anything'?" Paloma called out from the door.

"If you'd started listening in sooner, you'd know," Nancy Z. replied. "But what do you think I mean by 'anything'? It isn't a difficult word."

"What have you been saying?" Paloma demanded.

"Paloma," Faith interjected, "I think you've got the wrong—"

"How dare you?" Paloma glared at Nancy Z. "What kind of story are you spreading?"

By then, all the women had stopped working. They looked from Paloma to Nancy Z.

We're a mob of meerkats, Faith thought. *Sensing danger, suddenly upright, eyes wide.*

When Nancy Z. didn't respond, Paloma stormed out of the room.

"Let her run away," Nancy Z. said.

"No." Faith went after Paloma to explain. She caught up to her next door in the billiard room.

"You'd think she would only be half as infuriating now that the other one is gone," Paloma fumed. "The two of them and their ridiculous River Heights Roundtable—they would have been happy to rip Bea's society apart."

"You didn't hear the whole conversation back there," Faith said. "Nancy Z. had just complimented Bea and told us that she admires her."

Paloma narrowed her eyes. "That's a new one. Why would she say that?"

"Sometimes the truth is a mystery," Faith said. "And speaking of mysteries, can I ask you something? What were you doing on the floor behind the Agatha Christie statue yesterday?"

Paloma clapped a hand to her mouth, but it was too late. She couldn't suppress a burst of panicked laughter. "Wasn't *that* ridiculous? Promise you won't tell?"

Faith gave a wary nod.

"My pet mouse is an escape artist."

Faith took a deep breath. *Do not stare. Do not be rude. Do not sound anything but calm.* "You brought a pet mouse with you?"

Paloma, hand over her mouth again, nodded.

"It's loose in the manor?"

"But not lost. Not really. She comes back to eat. She just keeps—will you watch out for her?" Paloma touched Faith's shoulder. "Thank you." She hesitated, then returned to the crafts room.

Faith sighed. Marlene was not going to be happy if she found out a pet mouse was loose in the manor. *But Watson and the terriers will be ecstatic.*

When Faith went back to finish her necklace, Paloma had put a piece of classical music on. The room was calm with the concentration of crafters working and choosing beads.

Eileen leaned close and told Faith about a text she'd just received from Seth, one of the part-time employees at the Candle House Library. "Seth saw the same young man following Ned again. The man went into Happy Tails, and Seth dashed across the street and snapped this." She showed Faith the photo.

It was Drew Stapleton.

Faith wondered why Drew had been following Ned. She realized she hadn't seen Drew around much in the last day or two. He wasn't at the trivia night. Neither was Ned. Then something else occurred to her. Could Drew have created an elaborate game to scam Ned in some way? She immediately chided herself for the ridiculous notion.

But Faith left the craft session early and went looking for Ned to ask if he was certain the letter he'd received was from his father.

But she didn't find Ned anywhere.

15

Lois stopped by the library after the craft session to show Faith her finished necklace. "It isn't really my style, but I enjoy trying new things and learning new skills."

"It's lovely," Faith said as she regarded the jewelry.

Lois smiled conspiratorially at her. "Also, I'm nosy. When you went after Paloma, it reminded me that she left the panel discussion too. First Vic left. Then Paloma left."

"What did you find out when you went looking for her?" Faith asked.

"I didn't say I went looking for Paloma."

"You didn't have to." Faith grinned. "You're here at the Nancy Drew Clue Colloquium, and you have an eye for real-life mysteries."

"*Followed* is such a loaded word. Maybe I was just hoping Paloma knew the way to the nearest restroom." Lois gave Faith an innocent look. "That was going to be my excuse if she got suspicious and asked why I was trailing her."

Faith laughed.

"But it turns out I'm not very good at following," Lois continued. "Paloma was already out of sight by the time I left the room. So I checked the nearest restroom. She wasn't there, and by then she could have been anywhere, so I gave up on a failing career as a bloodhound and went back to hear the rest of the panel." She sighed. "There's another useless detail for your collection."

"And this might be another useless detail," Faith said. "But Marlene noticed that Paloma was absent Monday night when Nancy A. was discovered."

"Some people stay away at times like that to avoid adding to the commotion," Lois replied. "Oh, I almost forgot. What did you think of the fireworks between the Nancies and Bea during the panel discussion?"

"Unfortunately, I wasn't able to get ahold of the video. It belongs to the colloquium."

"Bea won't let you have access?"

"There's been so much going on that I haven't had the chance to ask her," Faith explained. "Besides, when I told Officer Rooney about the video, she said that watching it wouldn't be the best use of her time."

"But you don't have unlimited time either," Lois protested.

"Not that it wasn't a good idea. And Officer Rooney had a good question that you can help with. Did anything happen during the panel discussion that strikes you as significant now?"

"When I returned to the discussion, things were getting testy between Bea and Nancy A. They were comparing and contrasting the original and more modern Nancies. Bea asked Nancy A. if she didn't think some of the more modern Nancies abandoned the vision of Nancy as the self-confident, persistent, independent young woman."

"What happened then?"

"Nancy Z. yelled, 'Friends don't let friends abandon Nancy.' Nancy A. answered, 'We've already tabled that discussion.' One of the other panelists tried to smooth things over by saying, 'We're all friends here, aren't we?'"

"Bea has tried to get that idea across a few times this week," Faith said. "Although she has trouble living up to it. Paloma definitely has trouble living up to it."

"And Nancy A. didn't live."

"Do you think her death has something to do with that?" Faith asked.

"I don't know," Lois said. "But I sensed that Nancy A. saw 'We're all friends here' as a challenge. Like a gauntlet being thrown down."

"Interesting," Faith remarked.

Lois shivered. "I suddenly feel old and ghoulish. It's odd and very sad thinking back over Nancy A.'s last few hours like this, knowing she would so soon abandon us."

"But not at her own hand."

"No. But whoever killed her wanted us to believe she did abandon her life." Lois shivered again. "I think I'll go up to my room for a little while."

"I'll walk up the stairs with you," Faith offered. "I want to check on something."

The cat did not believe in abdication. It was his duty to accompany his human and the elderly female when they crept catlike up the wide stairway to the corridor where other humans went to nap and snore.

The cat modeled for his human the optimal posture—low to the floor, sinews and muscles coordinated with the litheness of a leopard. He demonstrated the appropriate paw-work—soft, sure, and quick, with the craftiness of a cougar. Alas, the subtleties were lost on her.

Still, he did not abandon the two. When they stopped and each put an ear to a door in the corridor, he tried to communicate that it was no use listening at that door for the sound of a foot, the whisper of a page turned, the sigh of a breath, or the beat of a heart. They would not hear those small sounds of life because their ears, although attached to their heads, were sadly inadequate.

As well, the human who occupied the room—he who walked in waves—did believe in abdication.

Faith knew she might be overreacting. There was no reason to believe there was cause for alarm just because she hadn't seen Ned since the previous afternoon. Castleton was a large mansion, and Ned was not obligated to appear for regular meals.

She made a circuit of the public rooms and stood for a time in the main lobby, reading e-mail and greeting guests as they came and went.

Cara, the desk clerk on duty, reported that Ned hadn't checked out. Then Faith spoke to Bea and Paloma. Bea said she hadn't seen Ned and she'd been wondering about his whereabouts.

By midafternoon Faith hadn't found anyone who'd seen Ned in almost twenty-four hours. She called Eileen at the Candle House Library. "I'm beginning to think Wolfe and I are the last ones who saw him."

"Maybe he's hiding out in his room because he's embarrassed at being caught," Eileen suggested.

"Lois and I listened at his door."

"Faith! Anyway, that doesn't prove anything. The doors are probably too thick to hear through. So maybe rather than hole up, Ned left without checking out. His room is already paid for, right?"

"That's true."

"Or he could be avoiding people some other way. I don't mean to belittle your worries, though. Hold on. There's a book here that might help." Eileen muttered to herself—a sound Faith recognized as the shelf-scanning mutter of librarians everywhere. "Aha. That's detective talk. I'm in the mystery section, paging through a police handbook for writers."

"Great idea."

"Here are the questions police ask when a person is reported missing: 'How long has the person been missing? Where was the person last seen? With whom is the person known to communicate and/or spend time? Why do you think the person is missing?' Does that help?"

"It helps me see that I don't have enough answers if the police ask me those questions," Faith replied. "It also made me think of another one: Why are you worried that this person is missing? And I do know the answer to that. Because there's already been one murder."

Eileen didn't hesitate. "Call the police."

Officer Rooney answered Faith's call and assured her the police would take the alleged disappearance of Ned Carson seriously. "Alleged because we have to be careful about making statements of fact."

Faith thanked her and hung up. For once, she was glad that the officer didn't offer additional information or tips. If Faith had reached Chief Garris instead, he very likely would have warned her to be careful. She *would* be careful, heeding earlier warnings from the chief, but without specific warnings for this specific situation, she felt she had a little more latitude.

She considered how she could verify Ned's story. Maybe she should first find out if Ned's father had actually stayed at the manor. With a determined step, Faith returned to the front desk.

Cara paused in her filing to look up and smile at Faith. "Is there something I can help you with?"

"Would it be possible for me to take a quick peek at the registration records? I want to check if a certain person stayed here about six months ago." Faith briefly explained the situation.

"Sure." Cara motioned for Faith to join her behind the desk. After she showed Faith where to scroll through the registration records, she went back to her filing.

Watson jumped up onto the desk, nudging Faith's hand that was controlling the mouse.

"You can advise, Watson, but leave the keyboarding to me, okay? We don't want to mess up the records by reserving suites for three dozen tabby cats."

Watson sat down on the desk and collected his paws prettily.

Ned had said his father stayed at the manor six months earlier. That should be easy enough to check. Faith started seven months back to give Ned room for error. She only needed a two-week margin, though. Six and a half months earlier, a Joseph Carson checked in, staying for a week in the Charles Dickens Suite.

Faith vaguely remembered a quiet man in his fifties who wasn't part of a group. He'd spent time in the library and asked a number of questions, most of which she couldn't remember. But now she recalled that he'd asked about the Nancy Drew Clue Colloquium. At the time, she hadn't known much about it. She'd found the information for him, and he seemed satisfied.

So maybe Ned's story is true. Or maybe he just knows that his father—or someone named Joseph Carson—stayed here.

While she puzzled, Watson nudged her hand again.

"Careful there. We just landed somewhere else—oh, wait a second." Faith scrolled down the new page. "You're cleverer than you think, Watson. I've found advance registrations, and here's what we want. Joseph Carson paid *then* for a suite *now*. The same Charles Dickens Suite, where he stayed and where we tried to but didn't hear anything last night. What do you think of that?" She held up her palm, expecting his version of a high five, which was a head butt.

Watson ignored her hand and hopped down to the floor. Then he walked away.

Faith sighed. *Being a stealthy detective is a lonely business.*

Still puzzling over what to make of Ned's treasure hunt story and now his disappearance, Faith walked slowly back to the library. She wondered when Officer Rooney or one of the others would arrive to start another round of questions and what it might mean if they couldn't locate Ned.

The colloquium program that afternoon was a screening of *Nancy Drew... Detective*, the 1938 comedy based on *The Password to Larkspur Lane*, so she didn't expect many guests when she unlocked the door for the afternoon.

Only one guest came in, and it was Paloma. She waved to Faith. Faith waved back.

Paloma browsed the shelves and chose a book. Then she walked over and sat down in one of the chairs near Faith's desk. But she didn't really sit. She kicked off her flats and pulled her feet up under her.

Curling up with a good book? More like tightly winding. Faith moved closer but stopped with a few feet still between them. "Paloma, how can I help?" She kept her voice soft and low. "Is there something you need?"

Paloma was crouched in the chair, her arms and legs drawn up tight. In a voice high and stretched to the point of breaking, she announced, "I need to confess."

16

Paloma reached out to Faith.

Instinctively, Faith took a step back, her arms rising into a position as though she knew some form of martial arts, which she didn't. *What do I do?* She took another step back and got ready to run.

Paloma dropped her hand. "I am so sorry. I lied to you. She isn't a mouse. She's a dusky-footed wood rat."

"What?"

"Oh my goodness," Paloma said, putting a hand to her heart. "I can't tell you how much better I feel."

Faith didn't feel better. She felt stuck in a loop. "She's a what?"

"A dusky-footed wood rat," Paloma repeated. "They're similar in size and general looks to *Rattus rattus*."

Faith gave her a strange look.

"*Rattus rattus* is the common rat," Paloma explained. "Taxonomically the two are completely different. And dusky-footed wood rats are much softer with larger, more rounded ears and a furred tail. You might know them by their other name—pack rat. They clean themselves just like cats."

"I don't think I've ever seen a dusky-footed wood rat."

"Here, I can show you a picture." Paloma pulled out her phone, flicked the screen, and handed it to Faith.

"It's so cute."

"She," Paloma corrected.

"I'm sorry. What's her name?"

"Bess. She didn't come back last night, and I'm terrified."

"Wait. What's their other name?"

"Pack rat. For the obvious reason. They collect things. The shinier the better."

Faith thought she might know where to find Bess. She didn't tell Paloma in case a tragedy had occurred, because she was pretty sure Watson knew where to find Bess too.

"Thanks for telling me about Bess," Faith said. "I'll be sure to keep an eye out for her."

As soon as Paloma left, Faith locked the library and dashed to the crafts room.

Watson suddenly appeared when she reached the door.

"Sorry, but I'd better go in alone. You stay out here and guard the door." Faith closed the door on the unhappy cat, then dashed to the cupboard where he'd discovered the shiny coins and the key fob.

In the dark back corner on the second shelf, she found Bess the dusky-footed wood rat with a small treasure of more coins, a flash drive, Bea's locket, and a nest of four baby wood rats.

Almost too late, she realized the crafts room door didn't latch properly. Watson had crept into the room.

He moved closer and chattered his hunting call.

"No way, buster," she said, scooping him up.

The look on his face clearly said, "Thwarted."

The cat was appalled when he learned his human could so easily be reduced to cooing by the hairless, squealing, tasty-looking, off-limits morsels. Mousles. Mice. But no matter. There was nothing in feline philosophy as enigmatic as human emotions, and he did not have enough lives to solve their riddle.

Instead, he drew upon his vast reserves of stoic discipline and climbed above the endless disappointments of human nature and missed snacks, the way a cheetah climbs a tree above the limitless Serengeti.

While his human put the miscreant mouselets under house arrest and returned the locket to the human named for an insect, the cat put his mind to the faint whiff of dog he'd detected on the shiny thing. Unlike mouse morsels, which teased cats by all smelling deliciously the same, dogs had their own distinct odors. The cat tucked the doggy whiff of the shiny thing into his memory and went hunting.

But the sheer volume of dogs and dog smells currently mingling in the manor were enough to block even the most brilliant detective, so the cat, like the cheetah on his tree limb, stretched out to clear his mind with a nap.

Faith slipped the locket and the flash drive into her pocket. Then she found a basket lined with cloth in the crafts room and gently set Bess and her new family inside. She rushed to Paloma's room and knocked on the door.

Paloma was overjoyed when she opened the door and saw what was inside the basket. "Thank you for finding Bess. And the babies are adorable," she gushed. "I had no idea she was expecting."

Faith smiled. "You're very welcome."

Paloma carefully transferred Bess and her babies to their cage. "I promise to double-lock the door of their house and throw away the key. Well, no. I won't throw away the key, but I will go into town and buy a heavy-duty lock that will make another escape impossible."

"There might be a market for the designer who can build a better mouse cage," Faith remarked.

"House," Paloma clarified.

"Yes, sorry," Faith said. "There's one other thing. When I discovered Bess in the cupboard, I also found Bea's locket inside."

Paloma sighed. "I was afraid something like that might happen."

"What shall I tell Bea?"

"The truth," Paloma said promptly.

"Good. I'm glad. Would you like to be the one to return it to Bea?"

"No. I'll have to face her soon enough, but I don't want to do it that soon."

Faith nodded. "I'd better get going. I don't want Bea to worry any longer about her locket."

On her way to find Bea, Faith rehearsed what to say. She fully expected Bea to demand answers, and she planned to give them. But she wanted to do it clearly and calmly—not rattled by Bea's buzzing.

Faith arrived at the salon as the film ended. She spotted Bea in the corridor and pulled her aside. "I have something that belongs to you." She took out the locket and handed it to her.

Bea smiled as she cradled the locket in her hand. "Thank you," she said, sounding genuinely heartfelt. "I was afraid I would never see it again."

Faith was surprised that Bea didn't ask any questions. "Would you like to know where I found it?"

Bea's gaze flitted to Faith. "The other half has been lost to me for thirty years, but as long as I've had this one, I've had hope. Half a heart, a vestige of hope. I had . . . I have another son." She closed her hand around the locket, turned, and started away.

Faith remembered the flash drive. She removed it from her pocket and called after her, "Bea, are you missing anything else?"

Bea kept going and didn't answer.

Faith returned the flash drive to her pocket. She'd give it to Marlene. She should be able to contact the guests about it en masse.

She felt a soft bump against her shin. She looked down to see Watson's upturned face.

"Have you forgiven me for whisking you away before we had another crime scene?" Faith bent to scratch behind Watson's ears. "I'm going downstairs to see Marlene. Do you want to come?"

"Your cat," Marlene said, pointing at Watson, "has been upstairs at night, teasing the dogs."

"He's usually home with me," Faith said, wishing she hadn't had to say the word *usually*. "What makes you think he has been?"

"I've heard three complaints so far today that *someone* is making them go wild and bark like a demented canine concerto."

"There is at least one cat staying here," Faith pointed out. *Not to mention an itinerant kleptomaniac dusky-footed wood rat.* "I'll make certain Watson is at home with me tonight."

"Be sure that you do," Marlene huffed.

"The reason I stopped by was to show you this." Faith held up the flash drive. "Can you find out who lost it?"

Marlene waved dismissively. "Put it in lost and found. My job does not include acting like the guests' mommy and picking up after them."

"You can't just e-mail or text the guests as a courtesy?"

"We don't do that. We can't do it for everything they lose. You could stock a flea market with what we have in lost and found. We didn't send out an alert for Bea's locket either. We have to avoid slippery slopes."

Faith thought that Marlene's avoidance might explain Bea's buzzing anger when the locket first went missing. It might also explain why Bea had just scurried away when Faith returned it to her. She most likely felt that attention from staff was too little, too late. "What if something's been stolen?"

"That's different," Marlene said. "Why? Is that what Bea's saying? Because that isn't what she said before. She very clearly said 'missing.'"

"The locket was found earlier today and returned to her."

"And now she's claiming it was stolen?" Marlene asked.

"I haven't heard that, but I don't think she will."

"We'd better *both* hope she doesn't." Marlene scowled. "It's bad enough the police are back asking more questions. I don't keep tabs on the comings and goings of every single guest. And it's not like the police have accomplished anything yet, except thumping around, thinking they're being so subtle. It's painfully obvious what they're doing, and all we need is for them to start another panic."

Ignoring the inaccurate description of Lighthouse Bay police officers thumping around with delusions of subtlety, Faith recalled the atmosphere at the manor for the past few days. There was the shock and sadness of Nancy A.'s death, but even Vic and Nancy Z. had held themselves together reasonably well. As far as she knew, no one had been unduly upset by the investigation. "Was there panic? I hadn't realized—"

"I assure you there was panic," Marlene interrupted. She looked as taut as a banjo string about to twang in two. "And I hate to think how the Jaxons will react to the headline 'The Case of the Killer Colloquium.'"

"It hardly bears thinking about," Faith said, hoping a calm, quiet tone would ease some of Marlene's tension.

Though it hadn't been a question, Marlene plucked each word in answer. "You've got that right."

Faith held her breath for a moment before bringing up the flash drive again. "Do you mind if I just make a quick announcement to the guests about the flash drive?"

Faith and Watson scurried from Marlene's office faster than a wood rat.

"That was a good deed," Brooke said after Faith told the guests assembled for post-cinema refreshments about the flash drive.

"Let's hope it's one that *does* go unpunished," Faith quipped.

"Are you talking about Marlene?"

Faith nodded.

"Then you need a prescription from Dr. Brooke for a piece of today's dessert—Tolling Bell Tiramisu."

"Marlene's under a lot of pressure, and my trousers will be too, if I keep self-medicating with your desserts."

Brooke laughed. "Well, I need to get back to the kitchen, but I've got news and a plan. Drew apparently hasn't been shy about telling people he's adopted. I'm going to use that as an icebreaker so I can get to know him—adoptee to adoptee. What do you think?"

"It's a great plan," Faith admitted, "but I'd feel better about it if we talk to him together."

"Sure. Why don't I chat with him about adoption and you ask him how he and his mother are enjoying the manor and the colloquium?"

"That's a good idea."

Brooke grinned. "It'll be like personal cop and not-quite-so-personal cop."

Faith grinned too. "So when and where do we meet with Drew?"

"I'm off at four. I'll offer him his choice of coffee shop or library and let you know."

Drew chose to meet them in the library, and he showed up at four o'clock on the dot with a vacant smile. He greeted Faith, and when she told him Brooke would be another few minutes, he wandered over to the display case. When Brooke breezed in, his smile took on some warmth.

"Sorry I'm late," Brooke said. "Is this kind of weird for you?"

Drew shrugged. "It's kind of a club, I guess." He looked at Faith. "How about you? Are you adopted too?"

She shook her head.

"Well, we can't all be so lucky," Drew said, and Faith could see that he meant himself and Brooke. "It's not all a bed of roses, but have you ever actually slept in a bed of roses?"

"No, thank goodness." Brooke laughed. "So how old were you when Bea adopted you?"

"I was a seven-year-old bouncing foster boy when we met at a church camp. She was the volunteer, and I was an 'uh-uh'—an adorable unadoptable."

"You've told this story before," Faith guessed.

"A few times. Mostly at church coffeehouses. Bea saved my life, pure and simple, and I owe her everything."

"Did she name you Drew?" Brooke asked.

"Believe it or not, my name was Drew before we met."

"That's so lovely," Brooke said.

Drew pointed at Faith. "Do you have any reservations about my story?"

Faith tried to hide her surprise at his blunt question. She shook her head, then decided it was time to change the subject. "How does your mother think the colloquium is going?"

"Okay." He paused before he admitted, "I've been staying close to her. She hasn't been feeling like herself lately."

"It's a lot of work, I know," Faith offered. "I'm so glad the locket was recovered. That has to be a huge relief for her."

Drew laughed. "The case of the anarchic adoptee—Paloma's wood rat, not me."

"Have you seen Ned around the past day or two?" Faith asked.

He cocked his head. "Who?"

"Ned Carson."

"Sorry. I don't know him."

"Where are you off to next?" Brooke broke in.

"Next? You mean, like dinner?"

"No. I mean, like a job," Brooke clarified. "Are you headed for grad school? Or maybe some big trip?"

"*My* future." Drew glanced at his phone. "I almost forgot. I have a call to make. I'd better get going."

"Oh, sure," Brooke said.

He waved to them as he walked out.

And when he was gone, Brooke looked at Faith and said, "Fake call."

Faith was preparing to lock up the library for the day when Midge stopped by.

"Congratulations," Midge said. "I hear you're an honorary aunt."

Faith gave her a confused look.

She leaned close and whispered, "To Bess's wood rat brood. I just made a house call. Everyone's in the pink of health."

"They're pretty cute too." Faith thought of something. "If Bess was out and about at night, would that set all the dogs barking?"

"Not last night. She was busy becoming a mama. Were they all barking?"

Faith nodded. "According to Marlene. She blamed Watson."

"That's strange. Vic only told me about Nancy A.'s dog barking. I suggested Togo start spending nights in the guest kennels. Vic and the other guests need their sleep, and Togo could use some TLC."

"Isn't Vic taking care of him?"

"Yes, but Togo's in mourning. They both are, and Vic might not be able to give the dog what he needs right now. A kennel might sound cold and uncaring, but Castleton's kennel is different."

"The poor dog."

Midge patted Faith's arm. "Don't worry. Togo will be all right. But you can't expect a bereft pet to instantly transfer affection.

Right now he's feeling abandoned. There. End of lecture."

Faith called Eileen after supper that evening. They chatted about new books and wood rats and laughed over Marlene's description of a demented canine concerto.

"I shouldn't laugh at Marlene," Faith said. "She's the one who fields the guests' complaints. In her place, I'd be high-strung too."

"No you wouldn't. Now let me tell you about my cybersearch for suspects," Eileen said. "Drew Stapleton has had a few sci-fi short stories published online. Seth read one and liked it."

"That's interesting. Did you learn anything else?"

"Bea has another son. Or possibly had."

"Her silver locket!" Faith exclaimed. "She started to tell me about the other half of the broken heart. She lost it thirty years ago, and she said she had another son."

"He got into some trouble as a young man, thirty or more years ago, and dropped out of sight." Eileen sighed. "Discovering such sad, personal information makes me hesitate to dig like this."

"You don't have to keep going. I think Bea has hope of finding him someday."

"But then I found out something that makes it all right again. Vic is a sweet guy, both literally and figuratively. He runs a fudge shop with his brother, and they donate 15 percent of their profits to charity."

"I never would have guessed that."

"Speaking of sweet guys, do you really think Watson was over at the manor riling the dogs in the middle of the night?"

"It's possible. I told Marlene I'd keep him inside tonight." Faith glanced at Watson, napping innocently on the sofa. "But you know his wanderlust. That only means inside here or inside there."

The cat, who had a superior understanding of music, briefly considered the possibility that a threshold number of dogs with the same name had been reached—a horde of hounds, a crisis of canines, a malevolence of mutts—and that made them capable of exerting undue influence over his human. Why else would she not snarl at the suggestion of a canine concerto?

The only way the cat could envision counteracting the criminal influence of lowbrow bowwows was to bring his considerable know-how and talent to the task of organizing an evening of much more elevated musical entertainment.

A cat cantata.

Friday morning, Lois, Vic, and Nancy Z. were waiting for Faith when she unlocked the library. Lois greeted Faith brightly, but Vic and Nancy Z. only looked capable of grunting.

The three guests headed for the chairs in front of the fireplace. Lois and Nancy Z. took the seats on either side of Vic. Faith joined them.

"They didn't sleep well," Lois said to Faith.

"I heard about the barking," Faith replied. "I'm so sorry."

"It wasn't barking," Vic said. "That problem has been solved."

"Tapping heels?" Lois asked.

Vic looked at Lois and hunched his shoulders, but he didn't answer.

"Don't be ridiculous," Nancy Z. chimed in. "It was worse than any dog."

"Wind in the chimney," Vic said. "It's nothing. It's September on the Cape. There's wind."

"And what? There are chimneys?" Nancy Z. said.

"Forget it." Vic got out of the chair and left.

Nancy Z. watched him go, then blew her nose. "I'm tired of holding that man up, but I've been doing it for Nancy A. Frankly, I have no idea what she saw in him." She blew her nose again. "I'm sorry for getting emotional. I'm just so tired."

"There's nothing to be sorry for," Faith said. "I apologize for the disturbed night. Did you hear anything, Lois?"

"Not a thing. I'm on the opposite end of the building, though." She turned to Nancy Z. "Did it sound like the wind to you?"

"No. Maybe. But no, it couldn't have been. It kept changing. It cried like a baby, and then it chattered like a monkey. Then it started making a horrible, low, eerie moan, and that was the worst—until it turned into a nightmare yowl."

"Are you sure it wasn't a nightmare?" Faith asked.

"That Vic managed to have at the same time?" Nancy Z. replied. "The only other answer is even more ridiculous than tapping heels—that I heard the Castleton Manor ghost Nancy A. teased everyone about. But what Vic and I heard was no joke. If it was, it wasn't funny. And there isn't a Castleton ghost, right?"

17

Faith attended to her work in the library that morning, telling herself she was being professional and competent, not hiding from Marlene. But considering how tightly wound Marlene was after the barking dog complaints, Faith didn't want to imagine—or witness—her level of stress if guests started complaining about a ghost.

She was glad to have the rolling cart to load with abandoned books and guests' questions to answer about the library's collections.

As she descended the spiral staircase from the second level with a book for a patron, she saw Wolfe standing at the display case.

After the guest left, Wolfe walked over to Faith. "I was wondering if you'd take a walk with me down to the beach. We can call it a business meeting and make plans to buy a new case with a lock that's worthy of the name."

She glanced around the library.

"It's all right. I know the owner," Wolfe said, smiling. "He won't mind as long as you aren't gone too long."

Faith laughed. "All right."

"Let's go out this way." Wolfe motioned to the terrace. "We're less likely to be waylaid." He waited while Faith locked the main door, then held one of the French doors for her.

Watson got up from his spot near the fireplace. He strolled over to Wolfe and rubbed against his legs.

"Hello, Watson. Will you be joining us?"

"There's no waylaying Watson if there's a chance for adventure," Faith said.

"Excellent. Lead on, Watson."

They crossed the lawn, following a serpentine walkway that took them toward the trees and the cliffs. Their talk followed the same kind of path, touching briefly on Nancy A.'s death, how guests and staff were coping with the investigation, and Ned's continued absence.

"I didn't know he was missing," Wolfe admitted.

"The police are looking into that too," Faith said. "But there's no great hue and cry, so I hope that means they've found him and I haven't heard the news yet."

"But you're worried."

"About the whole thing," Faith said. "I'm sorry. I don't mean to complain."

"Worrying isn't complaining. And please don't let the missing map add to the worries. It's not like it's worth anything. It isn't terribly quaint, for that matter. It's a child's drawing, and to be honest, my father wasn't that talented."

"Now you're just trying to make me feel better by maligning your father. The map is adorable, and he was very talented for—"

"An eight-year-old?" Wolfe finished.

"Absolutely."

"When we do find the map, I'd like to check something. I've been working on an idea involving it."

"Then I'd like to hear it."

"When we're down those treacherous stairs and on the beach. It's a good thinking place."

Faith laughed. "Logical and mysterious at the same time."

"I thought you'd like that," Wolfe said, smiling.

Watson walked ahead of them into the woods, only stopping to sniff the breeze before starting down the steep stairway to the sand below.

"He's pretty fearless, isn't he?" Wolfe said.

"What he lacks in tail, he makes up for in courage and attitude."

Wolfe went down the stairs ahead of Faith, telling her she'd be safer that way—if he tripped and fell he wouldn't land on her.

At the bottom, Wolfe raised a hand to his brow, scanning the horizon. "No luck. I thought I might see Watson riding on the back of a codfish."

"Watson's over there, enjoying your joke."

"He's found the fire pit. A fire on the beach is even better for thinking, and look, Watson's already stirring the ashes for us." Wolfe started picking up small pieces of driftwood.

Watson isn't stirring. He's staring. With a pair of glasses, he could be reading.

Faith approached the cat. "What have you got there?" She put her hands on her knees and leaned over to get a better look, then sank all the way down to the sand to sit beside Watson.

There was a partially burned letter in the fire pit. And it was on top of a stack of other personal papers. She could make out the ghosts of words on some of the burned papers. *Who set fire to them? And why like this?*

Faith reached out to touch the letter, to pick it up. But as she examined the letter, she realized it belonged to Nancy A., so she yanked her hand back. *Nancy A. is gone. The letter is almost but not quite gone. Why didn't the person who did this burn it all to ashes?*

Wolfe came over, his hands full of sticks. He dropped the sticks and sat down next to her. "Is there something wrong?" he asked, studying Faith.

She told him about the letter and other papers in the fire pit, then shuddered. "All those burned words feel like a funeral pyre."

Watson seemed to grow tired of staring into the fire pit. He stretched, then sauntered away.

Faith called the police. When Officer Rooney got on the line, Faith said, "I found Nancy Allerton's letter. It's partially burned but recognizable. There are other papers here too. Personal papers, not newspapers . . . Sure, we'll wait for you here . . . Wolfe Jaxon." She disconnected, blew out a breath, and looked at Wolfe. "Officer Rooney was glad to know it's you here and not a party of beach blanket amateur sleuths. Her words."

Wolfe gestured to the fire pit. "I wonder why these papers weren't destroyed completely. Was someone interrupted during the act?"

"If so, why didn't the person come back later to finish?" Faith asked.

By the time Officer Rooney came down the stairs, Faith and Wolfe had already discussed several more theories. They told Officer Rooney what little they could and then left her to her work.

"I hope whatever she finds helps to speed the investigation along," Wolfe said to Faith as they climbed the steps.

At the top of the cliff, they met half a dozen colloquium guests craning their necks to get a better view of the beach. Lois sat on one of the benches, and Watson sat beside her.

"Officer Rooney shooed us away," Lois explained. "Has there been a break in the case?"

"The police are still investigating," Wolfe said. "They'll make a statement when they're ready."

"In other words," one of the women said, "there's nothing to see here. Let's go back." She brushed past Drew, where he'd just emerged on the path from the woods.

"Nothing to see where?" Drew asked, glancing around. "What's going on?"

"The case of the clues at the bottom of the cliff," the woman called over her shoulder.

Drew stared at the cliff edge.

For a second, Faith noticed something familiar in his expression. *Where have I seen that look before?*

Wolfe pulled her out of her thoughts when he asked, "Are you coming?"

Faith nodded, and they set off again.

Watson caught up with them in the woods, then stopped to chatter at a squirrel. When Faith told him no squirrels, he swaggered ahead of them.

That's where I saw that look before—on Watson's face in the crafts room with the baby wood rats. And that was the same look she'd seen on Drew's face: thwarted.

When Faith got home, she called Eileen and asked if yet another book club meeting could be arranged.

"I know it's short notice," Faith said, "but—"

"I'll call the others."

The cat gazed at the humans who were assembled for what they called their "book club." But he knew that in reality they were gathered for his fan club.

He pondered his next pounce. On one paw, he now knew which dog's scent lingered on the shiny thing. On the other paw, he knew his human would not be able to read that clue. She was a dear creature and more catlike than most, but she had human limitations.

This sad truth would have depressed a cat of lesser character, keeping him from forward progress or possibly from investigating at all. That, of course, was not the case for a cat who understood the difference between one paw and another, a cat who still had a trick or two up his elegant fur tuxedo sleeve.

Whereas the cat did not believe in abdication, he did believe in abandon, and that was where he went now. He caught his human's attention with a seismic leap toward the stratosphere that made humans in their blinkered view exclaim, "What on earth?" Reaching maximum height, he threw the switch, power-cycling all over the room.

The cat power-cycled with such vigor, such ardor, such fur-vor, such splendor! He power-cycled with enough energized abandon to run the universe, which, after all, was the dream of every cat.

"What on earth?" Midge laughed when Watson suddenly leaped straight into the air and started racing around the room.

"Has he abandoned his senses?" Eileen asked, grabbing her teacup.

Faith held tight to her own cup and saucer, sure her eyes must have been as big as saucers over the sudden lunacy of her cat. "What did you say?"

"I'll rephrase it," Eileen replied. "He *has* abandoned his senses."

While Watson continued circling the room, bouncing off chairs and making the other women dodge and shriek, Faith reached carefully for her notebook, hoping to avoid flying paws.

"Sudden brainstorm?" Brooke asked, watching Faith successfully pull the notebook to safety.

"A brain sprinkle, anyway." Faith took out a pen and jotted down some notes.

Watson suddenly stopped his cavorting and jumped onto Faith's lap.

"Oh, hello." She scratched behind his ears. "Did you get that out of your system?"

Watson nudged her hand, then curled into a purring ball.

"Have any of you noticed the word *abandon* coming up a lot this week?" Faith turned to Midge. "You said Nancy A.'s dog is feeling abandoned."

"Yes, he is. Vic might not be able to give Togo the attention he needs right now," Midge said. "But Nancy Z. is spending more time with him, so I'm sure that's helping."

Then Faith told them about Watson's discovery of the abandoned fire on the beach.

"That's strange," Eileen remarked. "It seems like someone was trying to destroy evidence."

"But they changed their mind halfway through," Midge added.

"Now back to our *abandoned* colloquium," Brooke said. "Can we count Ned? They haven't found him yet, have they? Maybe he abandoned the event."

"But why?" Faith asked.

"We aren't dealing with whys right now," Brooke answered. "Let's give our report on Drew. It fits right in, because he's trying to figure out who he is as a person. He might have unresolved abandonment issues from before his adoption. Remember he was seven when Bea adopted him."

"You got all that from our short talk? I'm impressed," Faith said. "I can see how that might be the case. He's still a kid, searching for his future."

"What's your general feeling about him?" Eileen asked. "I've hardly seen him to know."

"I like him well enough," Brooke said. "He's rather easy to talk to. The only time he got tense was when Faith asked him how Bea thinks the colloquium is going."

"He just said okay and he's been sticking close to her because she hasn't been feeling like herself," Faith put in.

"And when we asked if he's seen Ned around, he said, 'Who?'" Brooke continued.

"Was he believable?" Midge asked.

"I had no reason to think he wasn't," Brooke said.

"Nicely sidestepped," Midge said.

"That doesn't mean he wasn't following Ned," Eileen said. "It only means he doesn't know his name. And before you ask, I found plenty of evidence online—records and images—of Ned being exactly who he said he is."

"I liked Drew well enough too," Faith said, "but here's why I don't think he's completely believable. He said he's been staying close to Bea, but that's not true."

On their drive back to the cottage, Faith turned to Watson. "I think you might know who's responsible for the so-called ghost at the manor last night. Hmm? Anything to say about that?"

Watson blinked and looked out the side window.

She laughed. "No comment. Wise cat."

When they entered the house, Watson dashed into the kitchen. Faith followed him and filled his dishes. She made a cup of tea for herself, then took her notebook and a pen to bed with her.

After she updated her notes, she read through them. Then reread them. Bea and Paloma disliked—or maybe even hated—Nancy A. Both were smart and capable. Bea had lied about knowing Nancy A. Drew was either protecting himself or Bea by saying he'd been sticking close to her. Vic might be a sweet guy at his fudge shop, but she'd heard him arguing with Nancy A. Nancy Z. thought he might be more in love with the car than he was with his Nancy.

And Togo apparently wasn't getting enough attention from Vic. Nancy Z. and Togo were mourning their friend. What did Lois remember Nancy Z. saying at the panel? *Friends don't let friends abandon Nancy.* There was that word *abandon* again.

Her eyes beginning to swim, Faith abandoned the notebook and turned out the light.

The next morning Brooke intercepted Faith and Watson before they could enter the manor.

"I could have called or texted, but somehow this seemed faster," Brooke said, bouncing on her toes.

"What's going on?" Faith asked.

"As much as I liked Drew when we were talking to him, I think it's him. I keep remembering the lie about sticking to Bea. It's a lie and an alibi, and it doesn't hold up. That makes sense, right?"

Faith caught movement in the corner of her eye, and she glanced at the parking lot. "And he's proving it again—he just drove past."

18

Faith and Brooke looked at each other, then sprinted to the parking lot for Brooke's car.

Watson was already sitting in the front seat of the red Miata.

"It's not the subtlest car for tailing someone," Faith remarked as they reversed and headed for the gate.

"But it was closer than your car, and it will be much faster in case we're lucky and this turns into a car chase." Brooke's eyes sparkled. "I have *always* wanted to be the good guy in a car chase."

She took the first few curves at a speed that swept Watson's whiskers back and made Faith question her friend's sanity.

They caught up with Drew around the next bend. For their first car chase, it was incredibly tame. Drew kept to the posted thirty-mile-an-hour speed limit and pulled to a stop in front of Happy Tails Gourmet Bakery.

"I'll wait out here," Brooke offered. "And I'll keep the engine running just in case."

Faith and Watson went into the bakery, where they found Drew talking to Sarah Goodwin, the store manager and Midge's most trusted employee.

Sarah greeted Faith, then gestured to Watson. "Here's our expert," she said to Drew.

He turned and smiled at Faith. "Great. I'm trying to choose a treat for Snowball."

"Tunaroons are Watson's favorite," Faith said, "but he also likes the shrimp whiskers."

"They sound amazingly delicious," Drew said. "I'll take some of each."

Faith bought a small bag of tunaroons, and then she and Watson returned to the car.

As they drove back to the manor, Brooke muttered, "What a letdown. Maybe Drew spotted us behind him and changed his plans. I still think it's him."

The cat appreciated the symbolic imagery of the trip in the sporty red automobile representing, as it did, the pattern of life. The ride began with the wild abandon of windswept whiskers (kittenhood and all it promised), segued into staid but steady progress (responsible, though sometimes disappointing, adulthood), and ended with treats (quite possibly heaven).

Let the humans debate the maybes and the maybe-nots of villainy. The cat knew better. Treats were always the plan.

Faith got a text from Midge while they were on their way back to the manor, asking to meet at the cottage.

Midge was waiting on the doorstep with a surprise when Brooke dropped Faith and Watson off.

Watson saw the surprise first and ignored it, walking right past.

"It'll be good for him to spend the day with you," Midge said, giving Nancy A.'s Togo a belly rub. "More socializing."

Faith smiled and scratched the dog behind the ears.

Midge handed Faith a shopping bag. "Here are bowls for water and kibble and a small blanket he can curl up on. He'll be happy here or at the library."

"How often do I walk him?" Faith asked.

"We've just been out, but he'll let you know." Midge passed the leash to Faith and grinned. "Have fun, you two. Gotta run."

"We *three*," Faith said for Watson's benefit when Midge was gone. She unlocked the door and stepped inside.

Togo seemed happy to explore a new place, but Watson hung back. "Oh, come on in," she urged the cat. "He won't be around for long."

Watson remained where he was and meowed.

"Let me know if you change your mind," Faith said to him.

She closed the door and immediately knew something was wrong. Togo was wagging his tail at something in the kitchen. Someone. And she smelled fresh coffee. She strained to hear a breath, the creak of a floorboard.

Watson knew, and that's why he wouldn't come in.

Faith reached behind her back for the doorknob. Then she threw the door open, tugged the leash, and slammed the door shut. She and Togo ran for the manor, Watson streaking ahead of them and beating them handily. Once inside, Faith punched 911 on her phone.

The operator asked her current location.

"I'm at Castleton Manor," Faith answered, then explained what had happened.

"Officer Tobin is nearby and on his way. Are you sure you locked the house before you left?"

"Yes."

"Did you notice any signs of someone breaking in?"

"I wasn't looking for any, but no."

"I'm not doubting you," the operator said. "I'm only collecting information to relay to Officer Tobin."

But the operator's questions made Faith doubt herself. Was someone really inside the house? Maybe Watson didn't come in because Togo was there.

"Okay, now that I'm breathing more normally, maybe there wasn't anyone. Maybe it was nothing or nothing but nerves. Except I smelled coffee." Faith didn't want to sound hysterical. Didn't want to *become* hysterical. She slowed her breathing again. "I smelled coffee, but I didn't make coffee this morning."

"Officer Tobin will be there soon. He'll be thorough. Don't go back to the house until he contacts you. Are you sure you're all right?"

"I'll be fine." Faith disconnected. She might be breathing more normally, but she still felt shaky, on edge.

Togo flopped down at her feet, and Watson blinked at her from a wary distance away.

Animals know. Watson does, anyway, and he's acting calm, cool, and collected. Togo might think everything's fine, or he might just be oblivious.

Faith texted Brooke. No answer came back. Brooke was most likely busy in the kitchen. Faith thought about going downstairs to see Marlene. *And say what? I got spooked. Will you keep me company?* She could go see Iris in the coffee shop. *No! No coffee. I'm sure I smelled coffee.* Instead she headed for her sanctuary.

Watson seemed to approve. As she unlocked the library door, he twined around her ankles. Inside, surrounded by books, she breathed deeply and finally stopped shaking.

Togo followed Watson to the desk.

Watson leaped to the top of the desk and looked down on the dog as though wondering what the library had come to.

Faith gave them each a few tunaroons. When she tucked the bag into her pocket, her fingers touched the flash drive no one had claimed. *Abandoned property. Should I report it to Officer Tobin? Or Rooney?*

She could hear Officer Rooney's reaction, her voice having morphed into Marlene's. *What makes you think it belongs to a current guest? It could have been left months ago. You're playing Nancy Drew.* Officer Rooney would be right on both points.

I don't have the answer to the most basic question, but I know how I might find it.

Faith sat down at the desk and fired up her computer. She glanced at Togo, smiling at her with his tongue out. "Sit."

The dog walked under the desk and lay on her feet.

"Good enough." She plugged the flash drive into a port—risky because she didn't know where it had been and what viruses it might have played with. But it was worth the risk.

When the computer finished recognizing the new device, she opened it to file view. She didn't immediately see anything that identified the owner. Most of the file names were simply strings of letters—*SOC, PLL, NML, WS, QMM, MMCM, HS, CTH, RHRT, GBH*. She opened a few of the files. They held a variety of articles, recipes, photographs, and newsletters—all of them referring to genre fiction or Nancy Drew. A number of the articles were written by Bea.

Faith felt a chill run up her spine. *Don't jump to conclusions. That's not proof the drive is hers*, she reminded herself.

Togo snored on her feet.

She went back to the list view and clicked *Date modified* to see which file the owner used most recently. At last, a file with a name that made sense: *Insurance*. But it was password protected. While she thought about it, she idly opened the next file down. *RHRT* held material about the River Heights Roundtable.

Faith's phone rang and she jerked, sending the mouse flying across the desk.

"It's Officer Tobin, Miss Newberry. How are you?"

As Faith retrieved the mouse, she got her breath back. Again. "Did you find anything?"

"I walked around the outside of the cottage, but I didn't see any signs of forced entry. Also, I listened and looked through the windows. I found no evidence of your intruder."

But do you believe me? She didn't ask him that. She didn't want to hear the answer.

"So, are you all right?" Officer Tobin asked. "If it'll make you feel any better, I can come get the key from you and check inside the cottage too."

"Yes, I'm fine. And thanks for the offer, but it's not necessary."

"I don't think you'll find anything, but let me know if you do.

You did the right thing by getting out of the house and calling. Don't ever hesitate to call."

"Thank you. I appreciate it." Faith disconnected, feeling thankful. She had Officer Tobin and the rest of the police force on her side. She had a handsome cat watching over her from the top of the desk, shelves of books in an exquisite library surrounding her, and a happy-go-lucky dog sleeping on her feet.

Faith sat up straight and refocused on what she'd just discovered on the flash drive.

If *RHRT* was a reference to the River Heights Roundtable, what about the other file names? She considered Nancy Drew titles. *SOC* could be *The Secret of the Old Clock*, *WS* might be *The Whispering Statue*, and maybe *PLL* was *The Password to Larkspur Lane*.

But as file names they didn't make sense. They didn't identify the contents. *Because they're jokers. Because it's fun.* Then why was one file different? *Insurance. Because it isn't a joke.*

Faith took a leap of faith. She clicked on the insurance file and entered a password—*larkspurlane*—and got in. There were two documents in the file—a life insurance policy and a draft of a letter. Faith scanned the policy, then read the letter.

To Whom It May Concern,

This is my insurance. In the event of my death, please run toxicology tests for substances on the list below. I was murdered by Nancy Zeigler because apparently she's more damaged than I thought. I know she killed me because friends don't let friends abandon Nancy, and if she kills me, that's what she'll think I did. I didn't, and I won't, and I hope I've convinced her.

There was more, but Faith hadn't realized how hard it would be to read. She stopped to take a deep breath.

Then she heard a low growl from Watson who was staring over her shoulder toward the library door.

She turned to look. Nancy Z. was coming toward the desk with two cups of coffee.

Faith's blood ran cold. She closed the document and stood up.

"Is Togo here?" Nancy said.

Togo came wiggling out from under the desk and wagged his tail.

"Who's a good boy?" Nancy cooed. "Would you like to go for a walk?"

"Here's his leash." Faith held it out, but Nancy still had the two coffees.

Nancy smiled and offered a cup of coffee to Faith. "For you. It's the least I can do after you've been so kind this week."

"Thank you." As Faith accepted the coffee, she wondered if Nancy Z. had been in her house. Was she the one who had brewed coffee in her kitchen? But why?

"It's a beautiful day. Why don't you come for a walk with us?"

"That sounds nice, but I really need to work," Faith said, hoping she didn't sound as alarmed as she felt.

Nancy gestured at the flash drive sticking out of Faith's computer. "Ah, but I really need to insist, because the thing is, a flash drive like that could belong to anyone. Even you."

Before Faith could move, Nancy yanked the flash drive from the port. "But judging by your reaction at seeing me, I think not. Several things disappeared this week, including this from my suite." She slipped the flash drive into her pocket.

Faith felt frozen in place.

"The key fob I left in Vic's room disappeared too. Any idea where that went? And with Bea's blessed necklace disappearing, there must be someone else here this week who's adept at opening locks. I wonder who." Nancy grinned. "We might like to exchange tips, and I could make a copy of that quaint but useful little map you so conveniently provided." She waved her hand dismissively. "Never mind. It's too late now."

I should scream or—

"Don't expect anyone else to wander in and interrupt us," Nancy continued as if reading Faith's mind. "Bea and Paloma have them all playing some silly game. Put the leash on Togo. Then we'll be leaving. You can enjoy a walk on a tall cliff. It's a ridiculously dangerous place to be."

Watson growled softly behind her.

Faith didn't move.

"Quickly. I have a gun in my purse. Even better, I have a bottle of something Nancy A. brought back from a trip to the Netherlands. It makes you sleep like the dead and really takes the edge off. Or sadly, in your case, it'll tip you over the edge of the cliff."

Watson growled again.

Nancy showed her the gun. "Come on. Let's go."

A gun. And all I've got—

Nancy waved the gun. "Move it."

Faith put the coffee down so she could snap the leash on Togo. The dog licked her hand, and she wanted to cry.

Out of the corner of her eye, she saw Watson reach out a paw and pat the hardcover thesaurus on her desk.

19

The cat gave his human the slow blink of conspiracy. He gathered himself into the coil of feline ferocity. He waited a millisecond for maximum suspense, and then he launched himself, hissing and spitting, over the dog and hit the floor running.

The dog, being helpless in the face of such magnificence and bravery, could do nothing but follow, yipping and barking, with never a hope of catching him.

Watson dashed away in a streak of fur. Then Togo tore after Watson, leaving his breakaway collar and the leash behind.

Faith lunged for the leash, intending to tie up Nancy Z.

"I still have the gun," Nancy reminded her. "Stop and face me. Put your hands where I can see them."

As Faith reluctantly did as instructed, her mind raced. She had to get away. But how?

"Good little librarian," Nancy sneered. "I knew you couldn't abandon your meek manners."

They faced each other with only the width of the rolling cart between them.

"We're leaving now, but wouldn't it be nice if this had a happy ending? Unfortunately for you, it only happens that way in sappy made-for-TV movies."

"It happens that way in *books* too." With a hand on either end of the heavily loaded rolling cart, Faith rammed it straight into Nancy Z.'s midsection.

The cart knocked Nancy Z. onto her back. She lay under the toppled cart, arms flung wide, surrounded by and partly covered with books.

Even though Nancy Z. didn't move or say anything, Faith checked that she was breathing. Then she pulled Nancy's wrists together and tied them with the leash for good measure.

She dialed 911 for the second time that morning.

At the moment the call was answered, Watson and a yapping Togo raced back into the library, followed by Brooke, Wolfe, Marlene, Vic, Drew, Bea, Paloma, Lois, and Ned. Vic caught Togo. Everyone else stopped in their tracks.

Watson leaped onto the toppled book cart and sat down to clean his paws.

Faith held up a hand to signal quiet and answered the 911 operator's questions. "Yes, I'd like to report a woman with a gun and a poisoned cup of coffee in the library at Castleton Manor. The woman and the coffee have been secured." She scanned the floor, spotted the gun under the display case, and upended a wastepaper basket over it. "And the firearm is secured as well. Officer Tobin answered an earlier call about an intruder at the cottage. You can tell him the intruder has been located and she's ready for booking."

After Faith disconnected, she looked at the mess of the books and cart on top of Nancy Z. and then at the silent gapers. "Although it looks like I've already taken care of the booking, doesn't it?" And then she burst into tears.

The police and an ambulance arrived. Wolfe and Marlene wanted Faith transported to the hospital too.

"But I'm not hurt," she told the EMTs. "I fell apart, but now I've pulled myself back together." The strong tea Brooke brought helped. She made sure no one touched the coffee.

"Nancy has a bottle of something in her purse," Faith told Officer Tobin. "She said it knocks the edge off and makes you sleep like the dead. I think you'll find some in the coffee she brought me." She pointed to her desk. "And a toxicology report might find the same substance in Nancy A.'s system too. That's probably how she got Nancy A. to sit in the car."

"You seem chattier than usual," Brooke remarked. "You might still be in shock. Or did you take a sip of that coffee after all?"

Faith shook her head. "I was suspicious when she brought me coffee, so I didn't drink any." She shivered as she finished her tea.

"I'll give you a call when we need you to sign a statement." Officer Tobin studied Faith. "Are you sure you're okay? Shock can sneak up on you in funny ways. You might want to take the afternoon off."

"I'm fine." She glanced down at Watson curled up in her lap. His slow, low purr helped her calm down.

"Don't push it, though," Wolfe said.

"He's right," Brooke said. "Don't make them take your book cart license away."

Faith frowned. "I don't really want to laugh yet."

"I'm sorry," Brooke said.

Faith noticed Ned standing off to the side. "So where have you been?" she asked him.

"Boston," he answered. "I was getting ready to return when the police found me."

Eileen burst through the door and threw her arms around Faith, making Faith cry again. When she recovered this time, she knew it was for good.

"You might think I'm crazy, Aunt Eileen, but do you think the book club—"

"If you say you're up for company, I won't argue. I wouldn't *dare* argue with either of you—the librarian and the lion. I'll invite everyone over to your place as long as they bring the food." She smiled. "Now let me walk you two heroes home."

Four old friends and a new one said grace over a meal of comfort foods that evening. Brooke chased Faith from her kitchen and made grilled cheese sandwiches. Midge brought herbed tomato soup. Eileen and Lois had made an ice cream run into Lighthouse Bay. Faith and Watson were the guests of honor in their own house.

When they'd finished eating, Faith told them about Nancy Z.

"She had two big issues," Faith said. "She was struggling financially because she'd lost her job, and she was struggling emotionally because she was losing her best friend to a guy she didn't like."

"How do you know that?" Lois asked.

"Nancy Z. told me about the job at trivia night. She worked for someone she called Goldie. This afternoon I followed up on some of those seemingly useless details. That was one of them. Goldie's is a locksmith company. Goldie Locks. Nancy Z. knows how to pick locks."

"I never would have guessed that," Lois remarked.

"I let Wolfe and Marlene know," Faith went on. "I hope they'll find the missing map in Nancy's suite. From what she said this morning, she took it and used it just the way Marlene was afraid of—to sneak through the passageways."

"She was struggling," Midge said. "But most people survive difficult times."

"Instead, Nancy Z. snapped," Faith said. "The Nancies were both single and such good friends that they'd made each other their life insurance beneficiary. If she'd gotten away with murder, Nancy Z. wouldn't have had any more money problems."

"Unless Nancy A. had already made Vic the beneficiary," Brooke pointed out.

"Nancy A. might have told her that was coming," Faith said.

"'Friends don't let friends abandon Nancy.' Nancy Z. said that during the panel discussion," Lois reminded them.

"That could make a fun motto," Brooke said.

"But it wasn't said in fun," Lois replied. "And remember what Nancy A. said next, answering Bea, but looking right at Nancy Z.? She said, 'We've already tabled that discussion.'"

"A bit of a private conversation?" Eileen asked.

Lois nodded. "Very much so."

"How did you find out about the life insurance policy?" Midge asked.

"It was in a file on the flash drive Watson found in the cupboard," Faith explained. "I think Bess the wood rat is responsible for a number of pranks like that, including relocating the key fob. If she hadn't done that, the police would have found the fob in Vic's room. Nancy said she put it there."

"How did Nancy Z. know there was anything incriminating on the flash drive?" Eileen asked. "How did she even know it was Nancy A.'s?"

"She knew Nancy A. and knew her habits, so she'd know Nancy A. kept records and files," Faith answered. "But Nancy Z. had no reason to think there was anything incriminating in them until Marlene read the note on that envelope. Then she couldn't take the chance. She didn't know she should be looking for a flash drive until I announced I'd found one. When no one claimed it, she guessed that was because it was Nancy A.'s. Vic didn't know enough about Nancy A.'s belongings to realize it was missing."

"But if the death had been ruled a suicide, Nancy Z. wouldn't have gotten anything from the life insurance policy, would she?" Lois asked.

"After a couple of years, a suicide clause expires. That's a handy thing to know." Brooke paused. "Or a dangerous one."

"Which was more important to her?" Midge asked. "Getting the money or being abandoned by her friend?"

"You can't really separate them," Lois replied. "They're plied together like yarn."

"Like twisted candles," Brooke added.

"Twisted any way you look at it," Faith said. "The mystery of the twisted murderer."

"I'm just glad it's over," Eileen declared.

"But I still have questions," Faith said. "Like what *were* the tapping heels?"

Faith and Watson were taking a walk the next morning when she noticed Vic packing up the blue roadster. Togo sat in the front passenger seat.

Faith went over to Vic. She felt like she needed to express her sympathy again. "I'm so sorry about Nancy."

"Thanks," he said.

"How are you holding up?"

Vic shrugged. "I'm taking it one day at a time. And I'm trying not to dwell on woulda, coulda, shoulda."

Faith motioned to the dog. "Is Togo sticking with you?"

"Yeah, I think we've come to an understanding." He smiled and put his hand out, and Togo gave it a lick.

"Well, have a good trip," Faith said. "Are you headed back to the fudge shop?"

"You know about that? I guess you would. You and your gal pals are the real deal when it comes to acting like Nancy Drew. So you know all about the tapping heels too?"

"That was you?"

Vic nodded. "I played a recording of tapping heels outside Paloma's room. It was a practical joke. I never should have done it. There's a shoulda. Oh, phooey. I did it for Nancy. I knew she'd get a kick out of it."

"What about the letter?" Faith asked. "Do you know anything about it?"

"I thought it was another one of Nancy's stupid jokes, and I was kind of out of my mind for a while this week. So I burned the letter—I never even opened it—and a bunch of papers and pictures of the two of us. The end. But after lighting the fire and tossing everything in, I regretted it. I couldn't bear to watch them all burn to nothing."

Faith didn't know what to say.

"I salvaged this picture at the last minute." Vic removed a singed photograph from his wallet and handed it to Faith.

She studied the picture of Vic and Nancy A. They were sitting in the blue roadster and grinning at the camera.

Vic took the photo back and returned it to his wallet. He smiled sadly, then got into the driver's seat.

Faith watched as he started the car.

Vic drove once around the drive, then stopped in front of her. "Tell you what. Togo and I will send you a box of fudge at Christmas. Superior grade."

Togo yipped.

And they were gone.

Faith and Wolfe were in the library when Ned arranged to speak to Bea and Drew.

"Does this have something to do with your graduate work?" Bea asked Ned, then turned to Drew. "You should take note, because this is exactly the kind of research you'll be doing."

"I've been doing a bit of research and a bit of genealogy this week," Ned answered. "It's been part treasure hunt and part mystery, and I'm calling it The Case of the Secret Prodigal."

"What do you mean?" Bea asked.

"I knew my father as Joseph Carson," Ned said. "He was a game designer whose final game brought me here. And the last clue led me to the truth—his real name was Carson Stapleton."

Bea drew in a sharp breath. "My son."

Ned nodded.

Bea wiped the tears from her eyes, then gave her grandson a hug.

"I don't know what to call you," Ned admitted. "I've never had a grandmother."

Bea didn't respond. She seemed overcome with emotion.

Faith grabbed a box of tissues and handed it to Bea. Then she hugged the three members of the Stapleton family—mother, son, and grandson.

Wolfe smiled and shook hands with the two young men.

Ned faced Drew and gave him a small, white box. "It belonged to your brother," he said simply.

Drew thanked him and opened the box. He held up a broken-heart locket.

Then Ned showed Bea the broken heart hanging around his own neck. "When I was in Boston for a few days, following up on clues, I had a copy made for myself so that Drew and I both have hearts that fit yours."

Bea still appeared overcome, but she managed to get herself under control before too long. She didn't take her eyes off Ned. "I am overjoyed. I cannot think of a more wonderful or fitting end to this colloquium."

Then her face clouded, and she straightened her already erect back. "But I have something to confess. When I said I hadn't met the Nancies before, I meant I'd never met them as members of the River Heights Roundtable. I did know Nancy A. briefly when she was one of my graduate students. We didn't get along any better then. But it was an unnecessary lie and unbecoming of the founder of the Nancy Drew Clue Colloquium."

"Don't be so hard on yourself," Ned told her.

Bea studied her grandson. "I think I must have recognized something about you. Perhaps that's why I haven't been myself lately."

"I was wondering why my mom was acting strangely around you," Drew said to Ned. "So I followed you around to see what you were up to. I'm sorry."

"I don't blame you," Ned responded. "I would have done the same thing."

"I'd like to apologize too," Bea said. "Drew, I'm sorry for being an unaccountably weepy old thing behind closed doors all week."

"*That's* why you were weepy and out of sorts?" he asked. "I was afraid it was because you'd killed Nancy A."

"Drew!" Bea exclaimed.

"I didn't want to believe it, and I never would have imagined you could do such a thing, but I've never seen you react to anyone the way you did to the two Nancies," Drew said. "I've never seen you hate anyone before."

"Oh my," Bea whispered as she touched her locket.

"When Nancy A. died, I felt jumpy, and I tried to protect you," Drew continued. "Maybe the Nancy Drew vibes got to me, but I wanted to make sure you had an alibi. You saved my life when you adopted me. I absolutely believe that. And I will save your life without hesitation every time I can. But . . ."

"But what?" Bea said. "That's no way to leave your mother hanging."

"But I do know Morse code," Drew replied.

Bea appeared confused. "What does that have to do with anything?"

Drew jammed his hands into his pockets and frowned.

It was Ned who answered. "I think he's telling you something you might have heard from my father too."

"And what are you talking about?" Bea asked.

"About being so sure that you know someone and that you know what's best for him that you lose track of *him*," Ned said. "And then lose him altogether."

Bea seemed to shrink. "I don't want to make that mistake again."

"And I don't want to go to graduate school," Drew said.

"But your writing—" Bea protested.

"Can wait," Drew broke in. "First, I'm going to follow another path you showed me through your volunteer work at the church camp. I'm enlisting in the army, and I'm going to be an army chaplain."

Bea wiped her eyes and gave Drew a hug.

When Drew stepped back, he smiled at his mother. "Don't worry. I'll get back to writing, but in the meantime"—he motioned to Ned—"you've got this guy."

Faith made sure to catch Lois before she left so she could say goodbye. That gave her a chance to say goodbye to Paloma too, because Paloma had offered Lois a ride to the airport in Boston.

"Thank you again for finding Bess and her babies," Paloma said. "I thought about offering you one of them, but with your cat . . ."

"Probably not a good idea," Faith agreed.

"I was going to name the babies after Nancy Drew characters, but Lois had a great suggestion, and if you don't mind, I think it's so much better."

"Oh?" Faith said.

"She told me about your excellent sleuthing this week, and I decided to name the babies Eileen, Midge, Brooke, and Faith."

"That's . . . that's . . . I'm honored, Paloma, and I'm sure the others will be too." Faith gave Paloma a hug, then turned to Lois. "I would love it if you'd come back sometime."

"That would be another dream come true," Lois said. "Do you

remember when I stood in your fantastic library and said that I could almost live here on air and books?"

Faith nodded. "I feel the same way."

"Ah, but after this week at Castleton and meeting you and your friends in the Candle House Book Club, I've revised that," Lois said. "I *can* live on air and books—with a pinch of mystery to liven things up."

Wolfe walked into the library one afternoon while Faith was taking the Nancy Drew display apart. Watson sat on the case supervising. They had found the map in Nancy Z.'s suite, and it was going back into the archives after Wolfe finished with it.

"I have the solution," Wolfe announced. "A harebrained idea has been racing around in my head all week, and I finally caught it by the tail." He glanced at the cat. "Sorry, Watson. I didn't mean to offend."

Watson blinked at him.

"It's the compass rose from my father's map," Wolfe said as he handed Faith the drawing.

Faith examined it. "There's a cat face in the center. Why didn't I notice that before?"

"We're working on new promotional materials for the manor, and I would like to see if we can incorporate the compass rose into them somehow."

Suddenly Watson jumped to the floor and began careening around the room.

"That's wonderful," Faith said, smiling, "and I think Watson approves too."

Wolfe laughed. "Someday he's going to orbit a room so fast he'll catch fire."

"He'll become a comet with a blazing tail."

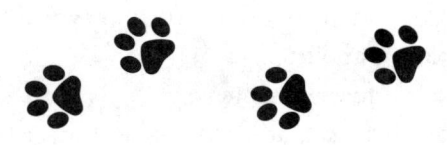

Despite his interstellar speed, the cat heard the humans.

So it was true! He'd always suspected he had a destiny among the stars. But not just any star—a shooting star. And not just any shooting star—a cat comet with a blazing tail.

At long last he would be reunited with the rest of his glorious, blazing tail.

YOUR FEEDBACK MEANS A LOT TO US!

Up to this point, we've been doing all the writing. Now it's *your* turn!

Tell us what you think about this book, the characters, the bad guy, or anything else you'd like to share with us about this series. We can't wait to hear from *you*!

Log on to give us your feedback at:
https://www.surveymonkey.com/r/CastletonLibrary

Annie's FICTION